THE COMPANY OF GOBLINS

Ple
on
Rei
w'

Other books in this series coming soon:

THE BROTHERHOOD OF THE BEE
THE LAST IDESA

To make your own goblin,
find more about Izzy's adventures
and investigate the mysteries of Teutonic Mythology
go to:
www.thecompanyofgoblins.com

THE COMPANY OF GOBLINS

Celia Leofsy

Little Knoll Press

The copyright for this book and its contents belong entirely to the author
Illustrations by Celia Leofsy
Cover illustrations by Michael Leofsy

Published by Little Knoll Press
First imprint – March 2014

ISBN No. 978-0-9927220-1-2

Copies of this book can be obtained from UK bookshops and online from www.LittleKnollBookshop.co.uk

Printed in Great Britain by Hobbs the Printers Totton, Hampshire

'We should try whether the prodigal might not be restrained from taking on credit the gewgaw held out to him in one hand, by seeing the keys of a prison in the other.'

Thomas Jefferson to Thomas Pleasants, 1786.
ME 5:325, Papers 9:47

1

An Unexpected Visitor

"Shh, don't wake the child," said a voice.

Orlando, the ginger kitten, stopped purring, pricked his ears and felt a tap on his nose. Startled, he opened his green eyes. The hackles on his back rose and he flattened his ears. Before him stood a tiny man, no bigger than him and dressed like a warrior.

"Who are you? What do you want?" he spat, readying himself to pounce.

"Be at peace, Orlando. I mean you no harm. I am Lord Falcon of the Ljosalfar, the highest order of elves. I need your help."

There was something about the creature's bearing, something about the way he spoke, that was reassuring. Orlando retracted his claws, and waited for the elf to continue.

"We have been watching over the child who sleeps beside you, since she was born. I need to know if you are willing to take an oath. An oath to watch over her and keep me informed if anything out of the ordinary happens."

"Why? Why are you interested in Izzy? She's only a baby. Is she in danger?"

"First you must swear. Do you swear, Orlando?"

"Yes, of course," said Orlando, becoming concerned. "I swear."

Lord Falcon smiled. "Thank you my friend. Izzy Green is a special child to us. I do not think she is in any danger yet, but we have enemies, enemies who may seek her out."

"What enemies? Will they come for her?"

Lord Falcon shrugged. "If we knew that, we wouldn't need your help." With that he bowed, the air shimmered slightly, and he disappeared.

2

The Silver Sphere

Izzy gasped – '*Nightwalker bared his fangs then sank them into the firm white flesh of her neck. She struggled briefly before submitting to his cold …*' Izzy hurriedly turned the page '*… embrace*'.

She was reading by torchlight, the covers drawn up over her head. Her large ginger cat lay curled up nearby, every now and then half opening an eye to check on her. Even after ten years Orlando took his duties very seriously.

Suddenly a shiver ran up Izzy's spine. She turned off her torch and lay silent, listening, straining all her senses. As her eyes adjusted to the dark, she could just make out a faint blue light through the bedclothes. She dropped her book, her heart pounding. She didn't dare look. She tried to stay silent, holding her breath.

Car headlights, it was probably just car headlights. She berated herself for getting scared so easily and smiled; it was half the fun after all. She ran her hand under her pillow, her tooth was still there.

"Now where was I?" she muttered as she picked up her book again.

Izzy was about to switch the torch back on when she noticed the blue light was still there. The glow slowly moved around the perimeter of the window, it was peculiar, it couldn't be a car. Her heart started pounding again. Perhaps there *was* something there.

Her curtains flapped in the breeze and she caught a glimpse, a flash of silver, just outside her window. She watched in fascination as the glow suddenly got brighter. It brushed past her curtains. It was in her room.

A silver sphere hovered towards her, its blue aura trailing a faint stream of light in its wake. It was small, no larger than a golf ball. Izzy was mesmerised, unable to move. Was she imagining it, was this real? The sphere got closer, lower, until it was right beside her.

"Orlando," she whispered. "C'm 'ere."

Orlando did not move. He was crouched in the hunting position, poised, hackles raised, eyes fixed on the object.

Izzy threw back the covers and shuffled away as far as she could. Her fringe felt damp where it was plastered to her forehead. She tried to call for help, but the sphere turned towards her. Her mouth was dry. No words would come.

A miniature trapdoor opened in the sphere and jointed metal arms swung out. In one of its metallic claws it clasped a note; the other snapped the air like a pincer. Izzy was paralysed with fear. Very slowly the arms moved towards her pillow, gently lifted it and slipped the note under. Then, as the arms retracted, she could see in its grasp, her tooth.

She finally found her voice and let out a piercing scream.

"DAAAAAD!"

Orlando suddenly made his move. He leapt across her and seized the sphere in his jaws. He ran for the window, heaved himself up and over, and disappeared into the night.

There was a scrambling noise from the next room, a squeak, and a heavy thump on the landing. Izzy's father hopped into her room rubbing his foot.

"What is it? What's wrong, Izzy?" he said looking around.

"There was something in my room," she gasped, "and it took my tooth."

"What? Where?" said her father, hobbling past the bed. "I can't see anything."

He crossed back to the door and flicked on the light switch. Izzy quickly threw her covers across the bed to hide her book.

Her father marched over, drew back the quilt and

picked up the book. "This is the reason you're having nightmares."

"Dad, I'm nearly twelve. Everyone's reading it …"

"Well, you're not everyone. And pick up Orlando's toys, I nearly broke my neck."

"Why won't you believe me? There *was* something. I saw it."

Her father frowned and ran a hand through his untidy brown hair. "I know you miss Nanny Ellen, but trying to get attention isn't going to help."

"All right – it was my last tooth and I put it out 'cause Nan used to do all that stuff, but this has got nothing to do with her. There really *was* something there."

"What's wrong, Tom?" Her mother's voice carried from the next room.

"It's okay, Liz. I'm just coming." Her father turned to go. "Settle down now, Izzy, and no more fairy stories."

"Wait. I've got proof."

Izzy reached under her pillow for the note, and read it out.

'Payment for one tooth, a dream to be delivered later,
dependent upon analysis. Conditions apply.
The Tooth Fairy.'

Her father laughed. "Well there you are then. You'll get a dream now instead of money."

"*Dad* – don't be so mean."

He chuckled, turned out the light and left. There was another squeak and a thud from the landing, followed by more grumbling.

Once her father had gone, Izzy was too frightened to sleep. She could hear her parents' voices through the wall.

"What was the matter?"

"Oh, just a nightmare. Did you know she was into

vampire books?"

"No, but they're going round at school."

"She's written a note to herself as well – from the tooth fairy ..."

"Probably because you've just cancelled our holiday," grumbled her mother.

"You know it's difficult at work right now. Anyway, she loves going to stay with your dad in the country."

"Still – that could've have triggered it."

Her father's voice rose. "I blame your mother. She filled her head with all kinds of folktales and nonsense."

"I thought it wouldn't be long before you dragged Mum into it."

"*And* she spends too much time shut up with that cat."

A tear rolled down Izzy's cheek, stung by her father's words. She thought about her grandmother and how much she missed her.

"Nanny Ellen would've believed me," she said softly.

She turned over and drifted off to sleep, tightly wrapped in her bedclothes.

"Night, night, Nan," she said, sleep-talking.

The shadowy figure of a woman with short grey hair stood quietly by the bottom of the bed. "Night, night, my lovely girl, God bless you, and keep you safe." She reached out and put her hand on Izzy's shoulder. "Listen, Izzy, the balance of nature is changing and you will have a part to play in correcting it."

"How do I do that, Nan?" mumbled Izzy.

"Trust your instincts. Trust Orlando." She rose and crossed silently to the door, gradually fading as she passed through it.

3

The Deal

Izzy awoke with a gasp. She glanced around her room through bleary eyes. Was last night really real? She paused for a moment, unsure whether to trust her memory. She surveyed her bedroom a second time, her focus clearing. Her messy pile of dirty clothes was still on the floor, her desk was covered in paper, as usual, and her posters were still hanging on the wall. But where was Orlando? An overwhelming urge suddenly took hold of her. She had to find him.

She dashed downstairs and ran through the house, but there wasn't a sign of him anywhere. She hurried to the kitchen where her mother was cooking breakfast.

"Mum, Orlando's been out all night. I'm worried, he never misses breakfast."

"I'm sure he'll be back soon. Cats can take care of themselves. Besides, porridge is ready." Her mother turned back to the saucepan and gave it a final stir. "And if he's not back soon, he'll get left behind," she muttered.

"I heard that. I'm not going to Grandad's without Orlando."

"You're in enough trouble already, young lady …"

The telephone's urgent call cut through the house and her mother rushed to answer it.

Izzy listened to her mother on the phone, her voice suddenly polite, overly sweet. It was her posh voice. Curious, Izzy went and stood in the doorway.

Her mother seemed intensely interested in whoever it was that had called. "No, no trouble at all, I'll tell him right away." She put the receiver down.

"Who was that?"

"Mr McAllister." Her mother looked strangely jubilant. "He wants you to go to the office with your father."

"What?" said Izzy, confused. Why would that make her mum so euphoric?

Her father hurried downstairs, doing up his tie as he came. "Who was that?"

"David McAllister. He said the head of your company wants to meet Izzy."

"Why does David want to meet Izzy?" said her father, bemused.

"No, Darling, not David, the *head* of your company … the head of the entire corporation wants to meet Izzy." Her mother was struggling to contain her excitement.

"WHAT? *I* haven't even met the man. What's the Chief Exec playing at?" Her dad was getting really quite agitated.

"You know he handpicks people for promotion, this could be an opportunity, Darling."

Her father hesitated for a moment before his face lit up with the same fervour as her mother's. "You're right; we can take Izzy to her grandad's later. You don't mind, do you, Izzy?"

"I'm not going."

"Yes you are."

"Not until I've found Orlando."

"Izzy – this is important to me."

"Well, Orlando's important to *me*," said Izzy.

She was still scared from last night, and somehow Orlando made her feel safe. She thought about explaining that to her parents, but after everything she'd overheard through her wall, she knew it would only cause more trouble.

Her father gave her mother a despairing look.

Izzy decided to change tack. "What if I come to the office first, and then if Orlando isn't back, you help me find him?"

"Okay, you've got a deal," said her father.

Everything seemed to be about deals since her father had started working at this new company. At least they'd promised not to leave without Orlando now.

Before long, Izzy was all dressed up in her best clothes and they were on their way.

"Why does your boss want to see me, Dad?"

"I don't know, we'll find out when we get there. It's exciting isn't it?"

They caught the tube into central London. The carriages were so crammed with commuters that it was suffocating. Izzy kept a tight hold of her father's hand until they got off. They walked through congested streets until they arrived at a building larger than Izzy had ever imagined.

"That statue gives me the creeps, Dad," said Izzy, looking up at the stone sculpture over the entrance.

"It's just St Onomans, the saint from whom the company takes its name," said her father. "Come on, don't worry about it, in we go."

Izzy stared wide-eyed at the grandeur of the foyer. The floor was adorned with highly-polished marble. It looked iridescent as the light streamed on to it through the vast glass exterior. She gazed into the expansive space above her. A gigantic spiral relief was sculpted on the ceiling far overhead. She looked down again, feeling slightly light-headed. She'd never seen anything so impressive, but it was also rather intimidating. She moved closer to her father and slipped her hand into his.

Near the lifts stood a desk, and behind it sat four

security guards dressed in uniforms of dark green and gold. Her father called a greeting to Marco, the head of security.

"Good morning, Tom. And who is this young lady?" said Marco, smiling.

Izzy smiled back. "Hi, I'm Izzy. Nice to meet you."

"Well, I hope you enjoy your visit with us," said Marco. He turned back to Izzy's father. "Mr McAllister said for you to go straight up to his office."

They walked over to the lifts, got in, and Izzy's dad pressed the button. The lift shot skywards, reaching the twenty-fourth floor in no time at all. As they walked out into a huge open-plan office, the glitz of the foyer quickly faded.

"Don't like this place much," Izzy muttered.

They walked past row upon row of desks. People sat completely expressionless as they stared blankly at their computer screens. They were like the zombies from her book, except these people didn't eat human flesh … hopefully.

"How can you work like this, Dad? No fresh air – no daylight."

"You get used to it, Izzy."

"No way!"

David McAllister's office was at the far end of the room.

"Come in, Tom. And you must be Izzy," he said, offering his hand.

She shook it gingerly. Then wished she hadn't when she felt his cold, clammy skin. Izzy forced a smile as best she could, but wiped her hand on her trousers as soon as no-one was looking.

Mr McAllister was a thin, nervous looking man, dressed in a black pinstripe suit. His bright red tie only served to enhance his deathly pallor. "Take a seat for a few minutes, the boss isn't ready for you yet."

"I thought I was flying out to the Island today, to work on the new contract?" said her father.

"That *was* the plan," said Mr McAllister, "but the chief wants to meet the families of employees that show promise as executive material."

Her father's mood lifted immediately and he glanced at Izzy with a look she knew meant, *don't let me down.*

The phone rang and Mr McAllister picked it up. He nodded, and then spoke to Izzy's father. "In fact, your timing's perfect. He'll see you both now."

Izzy followed her father and Mr McAllister as they made their way back to the lift.

"Hold tight, Izzy," said Mr McAllister as he pressed the button for the penthouse suite. "We're going up to the sixty-sixth floor."

4

A Strange Meeting

When the doors of the lift opened, Izzy shivered in the draft of cold air that hit her. Huge stone monoliths lined the way across to an enormous mahogany desk. In between were scattered expensive silk rugs, but they did little to soften the feel of the hard floor as they walked down the room.

"This place gives me the creeps, Dad," whispered Izzy.

"Don't worry, Pumpkin, it's designed to give the impression of power."

Then she saw the view and ran over to the window, "Dad, wow! Look, you can see the whole of London. And there's a helicopter on the roof as well."

She looked back into the room and lowered her voice again. "Have you noticed, Dad? There's not one living thing up here."

"What do you mean?"

"No plants, no fish tanks, just those horrible stones, it's like a cave."

"Mmm, they do look a bit ominous, I suppose."

"Tom, Izzy, please come and sit over here," called Mr McAllister who had been busy fiddling with some controls on the desk.

Izzy sank into a large leather armchair. She looked around, waiting for her father's boss to arrive. After a few moments a screen slowly rose out of the desk, displaying the image of St Onomans. She had the feeling it was staring at her.

A travelogue type of jingle began playing and what can

only be described as a commercial started. It showed the benefits the company's products would bring, and droned on and on.

Izzy shifted uncomfortably in her large chair; somehow she didn't feel safe up here.

"Sit still, Izzy," said her father.

"Sorry, Dad. I just want to see your boss and get back home."

"Actually, you won't be seeing him," said Mr McAllister. "Didn't I explain? This will be a videoconference. It's how big business is run, Izzy. The head of a global corporation like ours is far too busy to be in one place."

"Like talking to people on the Internet, Mr McAllister?"

"Yes. A bit like that, Izzy."

He leaned over to her father. "Actually no one sees KFC. Rumours were he had an accident or something and became a recluse. The shareholders don't really care as long as profits keep rising."

"KFC?" said Izzy's father.

"His initials. I'll explain later."

The video finally came to an end and the screen went back to the image of St Onomans.

A harsh, guttural voice came through the speakers.

"Good morning, David, Tom, and of course we mustn't forget Miss Green. I'm so pleased to meet you at last."

Izzy could hardly make out what was being said, his accent was so bizarre, like nothing she had heard before.

"Good morning, sir." Izzy glanced around the room feeling uneasy; there was only the picture of St Onomans to look at.

"Now tell me, young lady," the voice was oily, sugar sweet. "What are your interests and hobbies?"

14

The question didn't seem right, what was this all about? She looked at her father. He raised his eyebrows and nodded, urging her to answer.

"Well I like animals," Izzy hesitated, "and anything to do with saving the environment," she added in a rush.

She heard her father groan.

"That's very commendable, Miss Green, I would have expected nothing less." The voice dropped to a whisper, "but I'm sure you still secretly believe in fairies?"

Izzy was taken by surprise. "I'm too old for that."

"You still put teeth out for the tooth fairy, don't you?"

She felt her face grow hot. How did he know?

"Yes, last night, but there was something strange in my room and …"

"IZZY, I'm sure the Chief Executive doesn't want to hear about that," said her father.

"NO. Don't stop the child …" said the voice.

There was a long pause.

"Tom," the voice was controlled again. "You've got the Island contract haven't you?"

"Yes, sir, I was going today, but you wanted to meet Izzy."

"This contract is crucial. You'll be in line for a bonus and promotion if you pull it off. An old lady is sitting on a property. She'd be better off if she sells. I want results."

"I … I'll do my best, sir." Izzy's dad wiped his forehead with his handkerchief.

"Good man. If you get a move on, you can be there this afternoon."

There was a click and the screen went black.

The interview was over and Mr McAllister got up and led them back to the lift, but just before the doors closed, Izzy heard the harsh voice again.

"I was right, it is her. This explains the missing

transmission. She doesn't believe, so they can't make contact, but we'd better keep a close watch."

"Sir. Excuse me, sir. I think the intercom's still on."

"IMBECILE! Perhaps you need a spell in the mines."

"No, no it wasn't me. I think you knocked it …"

The lift doors closed and Izzy looked up at her father, then at Mr McAllister. They stood talking to each other as if nothing had happened.

Izzy followed her father back to his office. He headed straight for the coffee machine.

"What was Mr McAllister talking to you about, Dad?"

"Oh, it was just a joke about the chief's initials. The other execs call him Kentucky Fried Chicken, his real name's unpronounceable."

"No, I meant all that shouting as we got in the lift. Did he say anything about that?"

"Don't worry about it, Izzy. It was probably about the old lady."

Izzy didn't answer.

"Look," said her father, "I'll show you my new project on the Island. There's going to be a marina, with shops and hotels. I'm sure you'd be interested if you knew more about it."

"*Dad!* You sound just like that commercial." She glanced briefly at the map and photographs. "Can we go now, *please*. We made a deal, remember?"

"That cat wouldn't miss breakfast," said her father with a chuckle. "I promise we'll find him, and then we'll get you to Grandad's."

5

The Scrolls of Alfheimer

"I was really looking forward to our holiday, Orlando. Mum promised to take me skiing, but what if that gets cancelled as well?" Izzy picked at a loose thread in her cover while Orlando sat curled up on the bottom of the bed, listening attentively. "Since Nan's been gone you're the only one who seems to understand me."

"I should hope so, I've been with you long enough." The voice was strange, yet somehow very familiar.

"Grandad?" Izzy sat up and looked around the bedroom.

"It's not him," said the voice.

"GRANDAD! GRANDAD!" Izzy screamed as loud as she could and, after a brief pause, she could hear the sound of her grandfather clomping and wheezing his way upstairs.

"What's up, child? Whatever's the matter?" Her grandfather quickly looked around her room. "Oh those stairs, let me get my breath back," he croaked as he bent over double.

"I … I don't know. Grandad, I'm frightened, I'm hearing voices. Will you look under my bed?"

Grandad Jim got down on one knee and peered under the bed. "Nope – no goblins or bogeymen." His knees creaked as he struggled to get up, and he scratched his grey beard. "I expect you just had a bad dream."

"I wasn't asleep," muttered Izzy as she sat clutching the bedclothes.

"Well I've checked everything. Now be a good girl and

go back to sleep."

"But, Grandad …"

"Look, I'll be up soon, and I'll be right next door. There's no need to be frightened." He closed the door and hurried off downstairs.

Izzy couldn't relax; there was definitely something strange happening to her. Perhaps she was going mad?

"Don't be alarmed. It's ME." Orlando got up, bounced up the bed, and butted his great head against her shoulder.

"GRANDAD!" Izzy shrieked again and pulled the bedclothes right over her head.

Her grandfather came running up the stairs again. This time he was clutching his chest by the time he reached her room.

"I can't … keep … doing this all night," he wheezed. "What is it this time?"

"It's Orlando … *he spoke to me.*"

"That's it, Izzy. You're taking this too far. I know all about your 'Tooth Fairy' nonsense. Go back to sleep." He closed the door and went back downstairs.

Izzy called after him. "I'm sorry, Grandad."

She started to wonder if she was hallucinating or something. The thought occurred that she'd better not say any more about talking cats, otherwise he might phone her parents.

She resolved to hold her nerve if it happened again, and pulled Orlando onto her lap and smoothed him as he purred loudly. "Perhaps I've been talking to you for so long, Orlando, that I expect you to answer. Yes, that's it. I'm imagining it."

"No. No you're not. I really am talking to you," said Orlando, looking directly into her eyes.

She put her hands over her mouth stifling a scream; then took a deep breath. "Orlando! C-can you really talk?"

18

"Finally, we're getting somewhere," said Orlando. "A spell has been put on you so you can understand me. Listen very carefully – Lord Falcon of the Ljosalfar is here to see you. He is one of the 'light' elves."

Izzy opened her mouth to speak, but Orlando held up his paw to continue.

"It is of the greatest importance that you believe. If you don't, Lord Falcon will be turned to dust … instantly."

"But elves and fairies are just for kids. They aren't real."

"You're talking to me and I'm a cat," said Orlando. "You believe *that,* don't you?"

Izzy sat and thought for a while. There was no way to deny that she *had* been talking to her cat, and *he* had been talking back.

"So fairies, elves, pixies – they really exist?"

"They're all around us every day, but hide themselves with magic," said Orlando. "Are you ready to believe?"

"This is so cool."

"*Izzy?*"

She nodded.

"It's safe for you to come out now, Lord Falcon," called Orlando.

The air beside Orlando shimmered slightly, and Izzy looked on with amazement as a man no bigger than her hand appeared.

"Isabelle Green," he said, bowing. "It is an honour to meet you. I had hoped to keep you safe until you were older, but there has been a development. Do you remember something strange in your room last night?"

"I knew it! I was beginning to think it was a dream."

"It was a silver sphere," said Lord Falcon. "The first one we've been able to examine; thanks to Orlando, our secret agent." He winked at the big cat. "Unfortunately, we haven't been able to get much information from it. We only know that the spheres are snatching the teeth before us. Children's teeth are the source of all our magic. Without magic, the consequences are unthinkable."

"What's this got to do with my safety? I don't understand."

"Because we fear that whoever is making the spheres could have found you."

"But, why would they want to find me?"

Lord Falcon looked at Orlando and hesitated for a moment.

"It is written on the last remaining scrolls of Alfheimer that a human child would be found, and that child would possess the power to restore the balance of nature. We believe you are that child, Izzy.

"ME! Why me? What power?"

Lord Falcon looked away, "I'm sorry, Izzy. I am forbidden from saying any more. You have the power to make many things possible, and that power resides in choice. If I said anymore it would destroy not only your choice, but the power with it."

Izzy sat perplexed. "So you can't tell me, I just have to trust you?"

He looked back at Izzy. "All I can say is that we are not sure what information the sphere has relayed back. You could be in danger. If you come to the Ljosalfar palace with me, the king will decide what to do. Has anything unusual happened since last night?"

"I had to go to work with my father to meet his boss, and that was *really* strange." She pulled a face.

"No, I mean anything supernatural or magical. It won't be anything to do with humans."

She shook her head.

"Good. Will you come with me, Izzy? Will you help

us?"

"But how will we get to the magical world, Lord Falcon?"

He chuckled. "This isn't a fairy-tale, Izzy. There aren't any holes to fall down or rabbits to follow. You are here already. Magic is all around us. I simply have to take you to the palace. It's not far – it's on an island just off the coast."

She hesitated, "I'm sorry, Lord Falcon, but I can't run away. What would my grandad say, or my parents? I'm already in trouble. And if I'm really in danger, I think I'd be better off with my family."

"You don't have to worry, I'd put a spell on your grandfather and your parents to make them believe you're all right. But you are mistaken about it being safer to stay here."

Izzy shook her head. "I need time to think. It's all too much."

"Perhaps you are right and it is too late now for you to make a decision. I will return on the morrow, we will talk some more. Meet me at noon. Orlando knows the place." The air around him wavered like a summer heat haze, and he was gone.

Izzy's head was spinning. She sat quietly for a moment thinking about everything that had happened, and then she smiled. "Now I can talk to you, Orlando, I want to hear everything."

Orlando held up his paw again. "There's lots of time for that, Izzy. We have a big day tomorrow and you need to rest. There is one very important thing though; that cat food you buy me, 'Mr Kitkins' … it's horrible."

6

Decisions

The morning sun lit up the deep pink curtains and a warm rosy glow was cast into the bedroom. Izzy woke, stretched, and looked around. Everything was perfectly normal, just like always. Orlando was curled up on the bottom of her bed, she could hear her grandad busy cooking breakfast in the kitchen, and the delicious smell of bacon wafted up the stairs. She was just beginning to think she'd imagined everything, when Orlando gave a great yawn, shook himself, and bounded over to say, "Good morning".

"Oh, Orlando, it is true, you can talk to me." She held his great head and looked into his large green eyes.

"Of course," he said, purring loudly. "You won't forget about 'Mr Kitkins' now, will you?"

"Thinking about food already," she laughed, "some things never change."

She jumped out of bed, and got washed and dressed quickly. As she was about to go downstairs, she noticed a letter on the floor. "What's this, Orlando? This wasn't here last night, was it?"

"I don't think so. Perhaps someone pushed it through the window in the night. What does it say?"

Izzy opened the note and scanned the page quickly.

*'Isabelle Green, we suggest you think very carefully before you have any more contact with the elves. Now they have contacted you, **SO CAN WE**.'*

She stood looking at the letter, her eyes wide. "Orlando,

what does this mean?"

"I'd say it was a threat." Orlando stood on his hind legs and sniffed the letter. "Can't tell who it's from though."

"I must show Grandad," she said, running downstairs.

"No, wait," called Orlando rushing after her.

"Ah there you are, child," said Grandad with a smile. "Breakfast's just ready."

"Look at this, Grandad. I'm really worried." Izzy held out the letter.

Her grandfather took it and shook his head. "I've had enough of this nonsense, Izzy."

"But, Grandad, *I* didn't write it."

"I'm going to have to call your father."

"No, don't, Grandad, please. Why won't you believe me?"

"That's enough, Izzy. Eat your breakfast, then go to your room."

"Okay, but I can prove it. Orlando, say something."

Orlando looked up from his bowl, blinked once, then carried on eating.

Grandad Jim's forehead went really wrinkly and his voice went very low. "Do as you are told."

Izzy had never heard him sound so cross. She ate her breakfast in silence, then went back to her room.

"I did try to warn you," said Orlando as he groomed himself balanced on the window ledge, one leg high in the air.

"Why didn't you *say* something? Fat lot of help you were."

"He can't understand me. You're the one with the spell on you – remember?"

"Well, what are we going to do? He's going to call Dad, for sure."

"You've got a choice. Stay and do nothing, or go with

Lord Falcon. But if your grandad does call your parents, this may be the only chance we get."

Izzy paced back and forth across the room. "I don't know what to do? Whoever sent that note is definitely up to no good, and we may be in danger." She paused, deep in thought – nobody believed her ...

"I've made up my mind, Orlando. We have to go."

She listened at the door. There was no sound of her grandad moving about. It was safe. She crept downstairs, and carefully peered through the window. He was pottering about in the back garden. She ducked back down out of sight.

With her backpack filled with bread, cheese, water, and cat food grabbed from the fridge and cupboards, she left, carefully closing the front door behind her. She went down the path and took one last look back at the cottage. Orlando's tail was high in the air as he dashed along the trail that ran beside the river. Izzy didn't delay any longer; she turned, and ran after him.

She only hoped Lord Falcon would be able to work his magic before they came after her, or, even worse, called the police.

Orlando stopped suddenly, and put his head to one side.
"What is it, Puss?"

"Shush. Someone's calling."

"I can't hear anything."

Orlando clambered down to the edge of the river and stood close to the swirling water.

"HELP! Help me!" A desperate voice drifted up. It was barely audible.

Izzy and Orlando searched for the creature. Then at last they saw him, a tiny figure being carried along in the current.

"It's an elf," called Orlando.

Izzy scrambled down the muddy bank, while Orlando snagged the tiny creature's tunic with a claw and tossed him onto a clump of grass beside them.

The elf lay gasping for breath. He looked like a stick of rock that had been stretched too far. His wings were waterlogged and he had a pair of old boots tied around his neck, which had obviously been dragging him down.

"Well done, Orlando," cried Izzy, clapping her hands. "Are you all right?" she asked the elf.

"Don't eat me. Don't eat me," he yelled between coughs and splutters, as he backed away from Orlando. He was waving what looked like a tiny saucepan.

"Don't be silly, old chap, I count many elves as my friends, and I certainly don't eat my friends."

The elf continued to back away.

"A-and you're a human child," he said, eyes popping wide open and staring at Izzy. "You're not supposed to be able to see me."

"It's OK, you won't be turned to dust – I believe in elves. My name's Izzy and this is my cat, Orlando."

"Orlando Farid Arsalan Shah, to be precise, my father was Persian you know." Orlando idly flicked his claws through half-closed eyes. "It means 'unique, brave, lion of the king'."

Izzy looked at him for a second. Was he really *her* cat? He gave her a wide grin and seemed to wobble his head from side to side in satisfaction. She collected her thoughts and continued. "As I was saying, we're on our way to meet Lord Falcon. He's taking us to the palace."

The elf seemed to recover slightly and sat up.

"You know an elven lord?" He ran his hand through his blond hair to smooth it down, but it sprang back up again like a dandelion.

Izzy nodded and smiled.

"Oh, manners, manners, please forgive my manners. My name's Gillie – Gilbert Golden Oak. I'm a wood elf from the Great Forest. I'm on my way to the palace too."

"How come you were in the water, were you going for a swim?" said Izzy.

"That's … umm … right. Yes, yes, I was just going for a swim." Gillie went red and tried to hide his miniature pot behind his back.

"With a saucepan?" said Izzy.

"Oh, this? Er, well not really." Gillie waved it around in the air. "I just needed some water for cooking. My friends are nearby."

"Well, I'm sure Orlando will help with that."

Izzy nodded to Orlando and he snagged Gillie's tunic again with his claw, lowering him back down to the stream.

"Fill up your pot, old chap, chop, chop."

Gillie looked as if he was in shock, but followed the big cat's orders without a murmur. Then Orlando swung Gillie back onto the bank and picked him up in his mouth like a kitten.

"Now, which way to your friends?" said Izzy.

Gillie pointed in the direction of the cornfield opposite the river, and Orlando trotted off with him dangling like a mouse in his jaws.

Izzy followed close behind carrying the little saucepan, excited at the thought of meeting the others.

7

New Friends

A wall of tall leafy stalks loomed high overhead as they neared the edge of the cornfield. On the ground, in the long shadows, a small depression in the mud looked strangely out of place. It had a neat row of pebbles surrounding its perimeter as if they had been deliberately positioned, and a tiny wisp of smoke spiralling from its centre.

As they neared the hollow, Izzy could see a tattered old crow standing over another creature, an elf. Suddenly, there was a buzz of commotion, the crow fluttered into a nearby tree, squawking furiously, and the elf pulled back a bow aiming directly at Orlando's head.

"Drop him right now, or I'll fire," shouted the elf.

"AGNES, NO," cried Gillie. "By the fruits of Quercus, these are my new friends. They've just saved my life."

Orlando put Gillie down, and Agnes slowly lowered her bow.

The young woman was more like a warrior than a creature of nature. With her bow and arrows, fiery red hair, and tunic made from strips of bark, she was like a Roman Legionnaire.

Izzy set the saucepan on the ground and, undeterred, sat down next to her. She held out her hand and smiled. "It's nice to meet you, Agnes."

"You can see me." Agnes gasped and shot an uneasy look at Gillie. "How can she see me? Unless, unless … our magic has gone completely."

Izzy could understand her panic. "It's all right, I believe

in magic. You're safe with me. My name's Izzy. Are you a wood elf, like Gillie?"

"I'm so sorry, I'm forgetting my manners again," said Gillie in a fluster. "Izzy – this is Agnes Ash, a wood elf just like me, and this is Russell … he's flying us to the palace …"

Agnes puffed out her chest. "Actually, I'm not just like you. I want to serve in the Royal Guard."

Gillie looked exasperated and shrugged his shoulders. "She writes to the palace every week."

"There's never been a better time than now," said Agnes. "What with all these rumours about goblins stealing the teeth, it could mean war."

"So goblins are stealing the teeth then?" said Izzy.

"Yes," squawked Russell, "goblin scum."

"Russell, Agnes, how can you be such Goblinists?" Gillie gave them both a stern look.

Agnes pulled a face.

"You can glare all you like," said Gillie, "but there's no proof whatsoever that goblins are involved."

"I agree," said Orlando, "I nearly broke a tooth on a strange flying sphere in Izzy's room, and Lord Falcon said it was made by dwarfs, not goblins."

"You know an elven lord?" asked Agnes in astonishment.

Orlando nodded, with the smug expression of half-closed eyes and a wry smile. "The king asked me to swear an oath to protect Izzy … it's nothing really."

"Well," cried Agnes, "I haven't been to the palace, or even *met* an elven lord, and you've been friends with royalty since you were a kitten."

Izzy was listening to all this with great interest, but suddenly noticed Gillie was rubbing his arms and shivering. "Are you all right, Gillie?"

"I'm just a bit damp, that's all." He started stuffing some dry grass under his tunic. "I'll be okay. I'll just sit closer to the fire."

"Oh my goodness," cried Agnes. "I hadn't noticed – you're soaking wet. You fell in the river didn't you? I told you to be careful."

"No, I … I was swimming and …" Gillie started to go bright red. "OK, OK, maybe I did fall in. But the mud by the river wasn't ordinary mud. It was extra-slippery mud."

"If you say so," said Agnes. "Here, take my camouflage cloak." She held out a battered old piece of cloth that had grass and mud smeared all over it.

"Umm, no thanks. I'm fine, really." Gillie shuffled closer to the fire. "Let's hear more about this elven lord, Orlando. Did he say anything else about the dwarfs?"

Orlando was about to continue when Gillie let out a yell. Smoke billowed from his shirt and he ran around in circles beating at the flames.

Agnes picked up the pan and threw the contents over him.

Gillie stood still. With all the grass under his shirt he looked like a soggy sponge full of water.

"You didn't have to do that. I had it under control."

"You've never had anything under control," snorted Agnes. "Goodness knows why *you* got the letter to go to the palace."

"Look, I don't know why either, but I did, so it's no use you sulking. Just because you go around dressed like a warrior instead of a wood elf."

"I try to better myself."

"Agnes, we're wood elves. We're not meant to be warriors. You wouldn't have all these silly ideas, if you didn't spend half your time watching T.V. through the ranger's window."

"Why should I be stuck as a wood elf, just because you're happy being a nobody."

"We're important to the trees, Agnes."

"Elves, elves," called Russell, "stop this quarrelling, please. Our guests would never believe you're the best of friends."

Gillie and Agnes looked at each other with dismay.

"Sorry, Gillie, sorry, everyone," said Agnes. "It's just that my dreams are important to me ..."

"I'm sorry too," said Gillie. "I shouldn't have said they were silly."

"There's no need to apologise, either of you." Izzy looked at Gillie who was making strange squelching sounds as he walked. "We really must get you dry. Maybe Orlando could wrap his tail around you to keep you warm."

"He smells like a chimney. How would you like to lick the soot off my fur, afterwards?" He tucked his tail underneath his paws and held on to it firmly.

"There's still my cloak," said Agnes hopefully.

Gillie reluctantly accepted; he didn't have much choice. He wrapped himself in it, and sat down – this time a safe distance from the fire.

"Do you think the dwarfs are behind things then, Gillie?" said Izzy.

"I don't know, they keep to themselves. But we shouldn't blame the goblins without proof. The only way to find out is to get to the palace. Perhaps we could all travel together?"

Izzy smiled. "I'd like that."

"Well, if you're all going together, you won't need my help any more," said Russell, getting ready to fly away.

"Oh, are you sure you won't come with us?" said Agnes.

"No, no, my dear, I must be off."

"Goodbye, Russell, and thank you," said Gillie.

"Shall we go then?" Izzy got up ready to leave. "We don't have to meet Lord Falcon until noon, but we might as well make a start."

Orlando crouched down and turned to Agnes and Gillie. "We'll go faster if I give you a lift." He gave Gillie a quick sniff before he let the elf climb on board.

"I could definitely get used to this," declared Agnes as she sat astride the big cat.

Izzy smiled as she followed Orlando with his passengers – this was fun.

8

A Different Perspective

The track that led across the heathland was overgrown with gnarled and twisted gorse bushes. Branching stems reached across the path, tipped with vicious spikey leaves. It was a maze of thorns.

With every step they tore at Izzy's clothes. She picked her way carefully between them as she tried her best to keep up with Orlando.

"Wait. I'm bigger than you, remember?" she called.

Orlando stopped and sat down. Gillie and Agnes slid down his back, and landed in a tangle of arms and legs.

"Give us a warning, next time," said Agnes, dusting herself off.

"Oops, sorry. Forgot you were there," replied Orlando with a grin.

Izzy pushed her way through to them, un-snagging her jeans as she went. "How much further, Orlando?"

"You should be able to see the start of the forest by now, that's where we're headed."

"I can see it. Just up ahead." Izzy wiped her sleeve across her forehead. She was hot from the sun, and annoyed by her slow progress.

"Are you sure you're up to this?" asked Orlando.

Izzy's hands were shaking, and covered in scratches. She remembered the note, and thought about the threat it contained. "Yes, we have to keep going."

Orlando set off again, with Agnes and Gillie each holding on to fistfuls of fur, and Izzy followed.

They finally made it through the gorse, but before they

reached the forest, a huge bank of earth stood in their way.

It surrounded the trees for as far as Izzy could see.

"Do we have to go over it? Can't we go around?"

"Come on," said Orlando. "There's nothing to it."

"Wait. I think I'll get off," cried Gillie, sliding to the ground.

"Chicken," snorted Agnes. She dug her heels in Orlando's ribs and he sprung up the side as if he was a greyhound.

Izzy tried to stop herself from laughing, the only time she'd seen him move that fast was when she called him in for dinner.

"Do that again, Agnes, and you'll be walking," snapped Orlando.

Izzy bent down and opened her backpack. "Here, Gillie, get in. I'll get you to the top."

She scrambled up the loose, rough earth and down the other side into the cool shade of the trees. Before she had time to catch her breath Orlando looked up and sniffed the air.

"This way, it's not far now."

She nodded and they set off once more.

Orlando wound to and fro, through the densely planted trees.

"Faster, faster," cried Agnes, "I've always wanted a trusty steed to ride."

"You're pushing your luck, Agnes," he muttered.

Suddenly, Izzy lost sight of him as he disappeared through a small hole in a thicket. She sighed. Where was he taking them now? She fought her way through the dense mass of ivy and trees, coughing as the damp and musty odour clawed at her throat. She crawled her way through, deeper and deeper inside.

"Oi," called a tiny voice from behind her. "This isn't

much fun in here and I'm getting hungry."

"Sorry, Gillie. I think we're almost there."

Just as she began to wonder if the thicket would never end, she pulled a branch aside and a small glade burst into view. It was bathed in bright sunlight.

Finally, they had arrived.

She pulled herself through and was surprised to see Orlando sitting down comfortably in the middle of a ring of toadstools.

"This will let Lord Falcon know we're here," he declared. "It's a sort of beacon."

Izzy helped Gillie out of her bag, and got out some bread and cheese. As soon as he saw it he started grinning widely.

"Is that for me?"

"It's for all of us, Gillie,"

"Oh, yes, of course. That's what I meant."

Agnes brought over some pieces of nut, and winked at Izzy. "I'd keep an eye on that if I was you."

Just as Gillie was about to take a large bite, Izzy quickly picked it up and shared it out fairly.

"Why don't you ever get fat?" grumbled Agnes, selecting a small morsel.

Orlando had his cat treats, not 'Mr Kitkins' of course.

After lunch, they all lay on their backs and relaxed. As Izzy gently stroked Orlando, she started to think about her grandad and her parents and began to get worried. Were they all right? She'd now been away from the cottage all morning.

Suddenly, she heard the soft sound of beating wings. She looked up. A fierce bird of prey spiralled down through the trees. On its back was a tiny passenger – Lord Falcon. He shifted his weight from one side to the other and expertly manoeuvred the bird with unbelievable precision. Agnes and Gillie both stood up to watch, their mouths open wide with amazement.

Lord Falcon swooped gracefully between the branches, riding on the back of his beautiful bird, the light shining through its feathers. Then, diving down low, the bird spread its wings and alighted next to them without a sound.

Lord Falcon jumped off, a bright red robe covering his glistening armour. He bowed low and hailed a greeting to them.

"I'm glad to see you, Izzy. I hoped you would change your mind. I see you have some new friends."

Izzy nodded enthusiastically. "This is Gillie, and Agnes. They're going to the palace, too."

Gillie bowed his head. Agnes smiled and waved at him excitedly.

Lord Falcon looked startled and turned to Izzy. "Will they be coming with us?"

Agnes rushed forward. "Yes, please. We'd love to."

Lord Falcon looked a little tense as Agnes showed him her bow and arrows. He turned to the fierce bird beside him. "Hunter, see if there is another peregrine in the area."

"At once, My Lord." Hunter took off as silently as he had landed, and disappeared up through the canopy above.

"Now, how long have you been away from home, Izzy?"

"Just this morning, Lord Falcon."

"Good. I will put a spell on your grandfather's cottage. It will alter his memory, and anyone else that goes there. Now you have left, they will not be in danger."

Izzy was still worried about them, but began to relax.

Lord Falcon strode over to where Izzy stood and looked up at her.

"Are you ready for a little magic?" He took out a wand

from inside his cloak. It was made from silver birch and inlaid with flecks of gold.

Izzy nodded anxiously and was about to ask what he was going to do, when he suddenly brandished his wand in the air and began to chant in a strange tongue.

A fine blue mist twisted and spun from the end of his wand and wound itself about Izzy – first around her feet, then right up to her head. She started to feel dizzy and brightly coloured lights flashed near her eyes. A tingling sensation ran up and down and all over her body. Suddenly the ground rushed up to her head with frightening speed. She closed her eyes and hoped it would stop.

Izzy staggered. "What happened?" she stuttered.

"I had to shrink you, so Hunter could carry you," replied Lord Falcon.

Orlando came bounding across, purring heavily and gave her a sniff. Izzy screamed and fell backwards into a pile of leaf mould. She sat up and glared at him.

"Don't *do* that, Orlando, it's terrifying – now I know what a mouse feels like."

She looked up. The trees seemed as if they were miles away and the bushes were as big as trees. She staggered again. "It's like being at the bottom of a pit – everything's so big ... How can you bear to be this small? It's awful."

Agnes rushed over to steady her.

"Agnes, you're bigger than me," gasped Izzy.

"Don't worry, it's only temporary."

Agnes was smiling, but she wasn't looking at Izzy. Instead, she eagerly eyed Lord Falcon's wand.

"Wow, I want one of those," she whispered, looking at Gillie.

"Will you *stop it,*" said Gillie. "I'll cut you a stick, like mine."

Lord Falcon held out his hand to Izzy. "The falcons are here now, we must go."

Orlando rushed over to stand by her. "You haven't made *me* smaller yet, Lord Falcon."

"I'm sorry, Orlando, we won't be taking you."

The big cat's whiskers drooped. "You can't leave me behind. I swore an oath to protect, Izzy."

Lord Falcon paused. "Well ..."

"Please, Lord Falcon," insisted Izzy. "I wouldn't want to go without him."

Lord Falcon looked thoughtfully at both of them. "Very well," he said with a sigh. "Come over here please, Orlando."

Orlando's wiskers perked up again as sat in front of Lord Falcon. Izzy watched as he shrank before her eyes. He staggered, just as she had done.

Orlando looked up at the sky. "I've changed my mind, I don't like this. I'm smaller than most of the things I used to hunt."

Izzy laughed. "Perhaps you'll keep that in mind. Anway, you want to come, don't you?"

"Yes, but I didn't know it would feel like this."

Izzy picked him up and put him in her backpack. "Look, you'll be safe in here."

Orlando poked his head out of her pack as she climbed up behind Lord Falcon on Hunter. Agnes and Gillie clambered onto Melchare, Hunter's old friend.

"Everyone ready?" called Lord Falcon.

They all nodded – Orlando pulled a face.

The birds soared up through the branches, up through the tops of the trees, and out into the blinding sunshine of the afternoon. Izzy had to shield her eyes, it was so bright. It was terrifying and thrilling at the same time. She felt Orlando move in her backpack as he ducked back down, grumbling that cats weren't meant to fly. But she was glad he was with her.

"Where are we going, Lord Falcon?" she called.

"Southwest, we're heading towards the coast."

Izzy held on tight. An excited shiver ran up her back. She couldn't believe she was doing this. The wind blew in her face and her hair – she had never felt this free. What would the palace be like? What would happen when they got there?

9

A Close Encounter

Izzy started to relax as she got used to the exhilaration of flying on the back of the falcon, so open and unrestricted. She gazed at the landscape below them. As far as the horizon it was like a giant patchwork quilt. There were fields of bright yellow, brown, and green, interspersed every now and then with a small copse of trees. From the ground she never imagined there could be so much countryside. Villages seemed to be swamped in a sea of fields.

As they flew on through the afternoon the scenery started to change. They passed over acres of natural heath and ancient forests, then rolling hills of lush grassland that rippled in the wind like waves. It wasn't long before small yachts and boats were just visible in the distance, but the closer they got to the coast, the more built-up the area below became. As they crossed the shoreline Izzy could just make out an island that was directly before them. It appeared suspended in a haze, caught between the open sea and the sky.

She noticed Agnes and Gillie, waving and calling behind her. "What?" she shouted. "I can't hear you."

"We've never seen the sea before," shouted Agnes.

"It's amazing," cried Gillie. "It's so beautiful the way it dances and changes in the light."

"I could fly like this all day," said Agnes whooping with joy. She held her arms out like a bird. "Look at me."

"Stop showing off," said Gillie. "You could fall."

Izzy laughed at the way Agnes was clowning, but

0

didn't dare try it herself.

Suddenly they heard the raucous shrieks of seagulls. The noise was horrendous, almost deafening. They were diving and mobbing another bird. It was a merlin, and it was carrying a passenger.

Lord Falcon turned Hunter, but Melchare was already closer. Agnes and Gillie followed the stricken merlin as it went down.

Orlando poked his head out of Izzy's backpack. "What's going on?"

"We have to rescue someone."

"OH!" Orlando suddenly froze.

"CLAWS," shouted Izzy.

"Sorry," he mumbled, "too much water," and he crouched back down.

The seagulls harried the merlin relentlessly, until it fell in the sea with its passenger. Agnes gripped Melchare with her knees and swung her stick. It hit the head of a gull with a thwack.

"Whoa, this is what I've been waiting for," cried Agnes. "A real battle."

Gillie held on tightly to a feather, wielding his stick with only one hand. He was trying his best.

"Well done, Gillie," shouted Izzy, as he managed to club a few seagulls.

"By the fruits of Quercus," Gillie shouted, taking heart, "take that and that, you horrible things."

Some birds scattered from the blows that were raining down on them. But a few were still soaring and diving on the merlin and its passenger. Lord Falcon wheeled and circled on Hunter, trying to scare the seagulls, but his first concern was for Izzy.

It was working ... they were driving the seagulls away. Gillie leaned over to check on the stricken passenger in the sea. Without warning, he lost his grip, and plummeted down.

"Gillie's fallen," yelled Izzy.

She watched in horror. He was helpless, his arms flailing. He fell through the mass of swirling birds, their beaks snapping. One gull grabbed his leg, another, his arm. "*Do* something, Lord Falcon," cried Izzy. "They'll pull him in two. They'll kill him."

"He's too far away, my magic won't reach."

The gulls lost hold and Gillie fell like a stone again.

"He can't swim," yelled Agnes.

"Please, Lord Falcon, save him," cried Izzy.

Lord Falcon didn't hesitate. "Very well, hold tight, Izzy." He turned the peregrine, pulled back sharply, and Hunter folded in his wings. "DIVE," he shouted. "Dive!"

The cold air rushed past Izzy's face as they sped headlong towards the sea. It was hard to breathe, even harder to see. She held on with all her strength, her arms felt as if they were being pulled from her shoulders. Her fear was only kept in check by the thought that they might save Gillie.

Hunter tore through the air. They were gaining. They almost had him now. Hunter's great talons were spread wide, ready to grab Gillie. But now the water was rushing up towards them like an enormous blue cliff.

Gillie crashed into the sea and disappeared. Izzy closed her eyes, fearing they too would slam into the water. Then she felt a tremendous lurch in her stomach. She was nauseous, dizzy, disorientated; she fought to keep her lunch down. When she opened her eyes they were hovering just above the waves, having pulled up at the last moment.

"Gillie, Gillie." She scanned the water frantically.

"Look," said Lord Falcon. "Look, Izzy, he's over there, still holding his stick."

Gillie was bobbing up and down in the waves, his arms flung over his pole, barely moving.

"Gillie, are you okay?" called Izzy.

Gillie didn't respond and Izzy began to fear the worst.

"I have him," a voice called up from the water.

It was a young elven woman, the passenger who had been on the merlin. She was swimming towards Gillie, struggling to keep her injured bird afloat at the same time. "Your friend is conscious, I won't let him go under," she called.

"Your Highness, are you all right?" shouted Lord Falcon.

"Yes. Thank you. But Regan's injured," said the woman.

Lord Falcon gently peeled Izzy's fingers away from his sides. "Claws, Izzy," he joked. "You can relax now, all will be fine. Princess Ornella has him."

He then put a small whistle to his mouth and blew twice. There was no sound. Izzy began to wonder whether anything was going to happen, but then a shadow appeared under the water getting larger and larger. Izzy's mouth dropped open as the waves were cast aside and a gigantic creature surfaced, its cavernous mouth gaping and water cascading out of it.

"Don't worry," said Lord Falcon, laughing, "it's quite docile, it's a basking shark."

The creature manoeuvred itself with a strange delicate precision, until it was under the swimmers, and then it gently surfaced, lifting them safely onto its back.

Gillie struggled onto one elbow and gazed up at the princess. "Are you really royalty?" he muttered.

"I'm Ornella, and I should like to know your name. You were very brave."

"My name's Gillie. G-Gilbert Golden Oak." And with that Gillie passed out.

Hunter continued to hover just above the waves with

Izzy and Lord Falcon on his back, while Melchare circled high overhead with Agnes.

"Will you be all right now, Princess?" shouted Lord Falcon. "Shall we go on? Hunter and Melchare are tiring."

"Yes, thank you, Lord Falcon, I can direct the shark from here."

10

In the Palace of the King

Gillie, unlike the others, didn't get to see an aerial view of the palace. Izzy gasped when Hunter flew over the shallows and rounded the corner of the small bay.

"Oh, Lord Falcon, it's beautiful, it seems to be rising right out of the sea," she said, still trembling from the excitement of the rescue.

"We're very fortunate; nobody ever comes here because the bay is owned by an old lady. You're lucky to be able to see it. Usually it's hidden by magic, but we're trying to conserve what little we have left."

"What are those four white towers?"

"The one with the silver and blue pennant houses the royal apartments, and to the left is the Hawk and Falcon Tower. The other two are ceremonial areas."

As they flew over the outer walls there was a swirling mass of activity below them. There were markets, shops, and all kinds of magical creatures bustling about the streets. The sweet smell of freshly-baked bread drifted up, and then acrid charcoal when they swooped over elves hard at work, beating swords and armour.

"It's wonderful. It's everything I've always imagined a palace to be," gasped Izzy. "But what about Gillie, will he be all right?"

"He will be well looked after, if I know anything about a kind-hearted princess."

As soon as they landed, Izzy was shown to an apartment in the Royal Tower. It wasn't long before Agnes arrived. They were both happy to be sharing a room, feeling overawed by the magnificent surroundings. Extravagant couldn't begin to describe the lavish decoration. Gilded ceilings, four-poster beds, the softest silk sheets; Izzy wandered around the room too frightened to touch anything.

Orlando had no such problem and jumped up on one of the beds, padding the sheets to make himself comfortable. "C'mon you two, a bed's a bed."

"Well I guess he's right," said Izzy, following his example and finally sitting down.

It wasn't long before there was a knock at the door and a fairy helper entered. She told them that Princess Ornella was looking after Gillie in her chambers.

"How is he?" asked Izzy, holding her hand out as Agnes rushed across to join her.

"He's still unconscious," said the helper. "But the princess herself is tending to his wounds. Please don't worry, stay here and rest."

Izzy and Agnes waited anxiously, sitting down one minute, pacing the room the next, or just staring out the window in silence. It seemed an age before they were finally told they could go and see Gillie. It was with some relief that they finally knocked on Princess Ornella's door.

"Come in," said Ornella. "We don't understand why the seagulls attacked, but you were all very brave, especially you, Agnes. You are a fine warrior."

"Perhaps ordinary elves could be royal guards then …?"

"Let's not talk about changing traditions now," interrupted Ornella. "I'm sure Gillie would like to see you first."

They entered the room, but remained by the door while Princess Ornella tended to Gillie. Orlando slunk past Izzy's legs, hopped onto the bed and circled around a couple of times before settling down.

"How do you feel now, Gillie?" said Ornella.

"I don't really know. My arm feels a bit better, though. Have I missed the council meeting?"

"No. It's tomorrow morning. But don't worry, my father will come to see you later. You're staying put until you're completely better. By the way, your letter of invitation was actually meant for Lord Goshawk."

"Oh, so it wasn't for me?" said Gillie, sounding disappointed. "I did think it a bit strange. After all, I'm only a wood elf."

"No. Not *only* a wood elf," said Ornella, laughing.

Gillie lay back, sinking into soft, silky sheets. He was mesmerised by the beautiful young princess. He couldn't take his eyes off her. He hardly looked when Izzy and Agnes came over to sit by him.

"By the fruits of Quercus," exclaimed Gillie, suddenly sitting up and staring at them. "You look stunning, Agnes."

Agnes went as red as her hair.

"I was *forced* to wear this. It's for the banquet tonight."

She was wearing a midnight blue gown with tiny stars, just like the night sky, with a sash of pure silver thread wound around her waist. Her hair had been combed out and left to fall in natural waves. It was true that she stood head and shoulders above the other fairies and elves, but the overall effect was quite elegant, although on a larger scale.

"You both look lovely," said Ornella. "And, Izzy, you could be an elven princess."

Izzy was dressed in pink chiffon that was sewn all over with the finest seed pearls. Her fair hair was braided and woven with tiny pink rose buds. She didn't let on, but she did feel just like a princess.

48

Only Orlando looked unhappy. Around his neck was tied a large red bow, and attached to this were two small bells.

Izzy smoothed his head and laughed. "I'll have to try that at home, I'm sure the mice would like it, too."

Orlando scowled. "What am I going to catch when I'm this small?"

"It's almost time for the banquet," announced Ornella. "Come, we should go and take our places. Gillie, you must stay here and rest, we'll pop in to see you later when you've had something to eat and you're feeling better." With that she swept out of the chamber and beckoned the others to follow.

Izzy and Agnes held hands as they walked along behind the princess. They pressed close together and neither of them spoke, their attention focussed on every sight and sound. Only Orlando seemed unphased, and he chased after the pearls on Izzy's dress.

When they got near the great banqueting hall, a low murmur could be heard. It rose up from the voices of all the great lords, ladies, and councillors of the king.

Ten enormous chandeliers dominated the room. They shimmered and dazzled with the light that caught their crystals. The walls were wood-panelled and covered with tapestries and paintings, many depicting ancient tales of valour and scenes of battles, others portraits of the king's ancestors. There was a long dining table set out with exquisite glassware and silver cutlery, and in the centre stood a magnificent candelabrum surrounded by rare and exotic flowers.

The guests suddenly became hushed and stewards announced the arrival of the king.

"I don't feel comfortable," grumbled Agnes, pulling at her sash. "I'd rather be in my own clothes."

"Shush," said Izzy, "the king's coming."

A tall, distinguished-looking elf swept into the hall. Izzy was about to curtsey, when she heard someone whisper it was the chancellor, Seraphino Cosmos.

Finally, King Thodrek appeared. He looked very much a warrior and there was no mistaking him as the king. He came over to Ornella and she dropped a graceful curtsey before introducing Izzy, Agnes and Orlando. The girls curtseyed awkwardly, and Orlando bowed his head. The rest of the assembly did the same, remaining bowed until the king bade them all welcome.

King Thodrek took his place and motioned for everyone to be seated. The fairy stewards came in and stood behind the chair of each guest, ready to attend to any need they might have.

The meal was sumptuous, with the most incredible dishes that could be imagined. But nothing could have prepared Izzy for the desserts. There were gasps all around when they were brought in. There were enormous cakes decorated with enchanted dancing figures, meringues, fruit, and sculptured ice swans that drifted above the table. Nestled in the swans' wings was every imaginable flavour of ice cream, from Madagascan vanilla and saffron, to chocolate fudge toffee.

Agnes sat toying with her food and looking grumpy.

"What's wrong?" whispered Izzy. "How can you be unhappy? It's all so amazing."

"I was just thinking about all the waste of food and magic. Wood elves would never squander resources like this. We have to be very careful because of the shortages, it makes me so angry."

Izzy was just about to say something, when the doors at the back of the hall were flung open. A young elven lord with jet-black hair, worn-looking travel clothes, and a number of weapons about his person, stumbled in. With formidable strength he dragged a guard on either side with him as he struggled down the chamber.

"Let me go. Your Majesty, *please,* I am Lord Goshawk and I should have received an invitation, but it never arrived. I only found out by chance and have travelled all day and night to get here."

The two guards fought to hold him back, but the young lord continued to drag them the entire length of the hall, until he stood before the king.

"You may be in danger, Your Majesty," he urged. "I believe someone is impersonating me. When I arrived I was told that a Lord Gilbert Golden Oak was already here with a Miss Agnes Ash, and I certainly have never heard of either of them."

It was all too much for Agnes. She marched around the table to Lord Goshawk, swung her fist and punched him full in the nose. He crumpled between the guards.

"Don't you dare slander my friend when he's not here to defend himself," she said. "An invitation was delivered to his home – I saw it. All that was left of the name was a golden G; the rain had washed out the rest. How were we to know it was for you?"

Lord Goshawk looked up through bleary eyes and a bloody nose.

"Well, bested by a girl," he muttered. "I spoke in haste, truly I apologise. I say, this Gillie is a lucky chap to have someone stand up for him like you just did. I'd deem it an honour to have you as a friend, too."

Agnes stood dumfounded for a moment, went red, then hurried back to her chair.

A wave of murmuring broke out in the hall.

"Order. Order," cried Lord Falcon. "Lord Goshawk, the king will see you privately in his apartments in thirty minutes. That should give you time to clean yourself up somewhat and attend to your nose. Now if the excitement is over, please, the banquet will continue."

Later that evening, Izzy, Orlando, Agnes, and Ornella were crowded around Gillie's bedside. He was sitting up and looking a lot better.

They sat around, some perching on the bed, laughing and talking while Gillie ate his supper. Izzy was annoyed because Orlando was curled on Ornella's lap, purring completely outrageously.

There was a knock on the door and Ornella jumped up to open it. Izzy took the opportunity to coax Orlando back to her, making sure he knew which lap he was supposed to be on.

The king stood in the corridor with Lord Goshawk. "I hope you don't mind, my dear, Lord Goshawk asked if he could apologise to Gillie in person for the misunderstanding."

"Yes of course, Father. Lord Goshawk, please come in."

Ornella made the introductions. "I think you've met Agnes already?" she said with a grin.

"My nose has at least," said Lord Goshawk, and made a bow to Agnes. He went over to the bed and held out his hand to Gillie. "I'm very sorry I misjudged you, I thought you'd stolen my identity. Please accept my apology."

Gillie shook with his good hand. "Don't worry about it, My Lord, it could happen to anyone." Then he looked across at Agnes, who had gone very red. "You didn't *hit* Lord Goshawk did you, Agnes?"

Before she could answer, Lord Goshawk spoke again. "Please call me Gavin." He threw a smile at Agnes. "I'd have done the same myself in similar circumstances."

"Well," said the king, "we have a big day tomorrow with the High Council meeting. It's time Lord Goshawk and I said goodnight."

"Goodnight, Father," said Ornella. "Perhaps we had all better go to bed now. It's been a very exciting day."

Izzy tucked Orlando under her arm, just in case he had any other ideas, said goodnight, and returned to her room with Agnes.

"Well. I can't believe the nerve of that Lord Goshawk," said Agnes, who was now simmering with indignation. "Making friends with Gillie like that, after everything he said at the banquet."

"He did apologise, Agnes, and he looks very strong. I bet he's a trained warrior. Did you see all the weapons he was carrying?"

"Humph," snorted Agnes, "I bet I can shoot arrows better than him. I've been practising splitting the arrow, just like Robin Hood."

"That's amazing, Agnes – he probably couldn't do that. I'm sure Robin Hood could show him a thing or two," said Izzy with a smirk. She put Orlando down on the bottom of her bed and he started padding the quilt.

"Goodnight, Agnes. Goodnight, Izzy."

"I'm never going to get used to hearing you speak," said Izzy laughing. She got changed into her pyjamas, silk of course, brushed her teeth and collapsed into the deep, soft, quilted bed.

Agnes did the same, grumbling about how silk was 'too silky' for her, but it wasn't long before they were all fast asleep.

"Night, night, Nanny Ellen," said Izzy, sleep talking again.

The figure of a woman sat on the end of Izzy's bed; she smiled and smoothed Orlando as he purred gently.

"Izzy, remember Cat Bells," she said, "dwarfs and Cat Bells. You must go to the dwarfs at Cat Bells." She blew Izzy a kiss and slowly disappeared.

11

Cat Bells

Izzy woke up early and got dressed. It felt a bit boring to wear her own clothes again after the banquet the night before.

"I wonder if we'll get the chance to dress up again," said Izzy, looking longingly at her party dress.

"I prefer my own clothes," said Agnes, plaiting her hair, "all those frills and flowers, it's just not me."

"But you looked lovely," said Izzy. "I think Gavin thought you looked lovely, too."

Agnes gave Izzy a furious glare, "Don't you dare start saying things like that. You know it's not true, I can't stand him."

"I'm only pulling your leg, Agnes, don't be cross."

"Well, I suppose he is reasonably good-looking," said Agnes, smiling. "But the bloody nose was a definite improvement."

Both girls laughed so hard the bed bounced up and down, much to Orlando's disgust, as he wasn't ready to get up just yet.

"Did you know you talk in your sleep?" said Agnes when they stopped to catch their breath. "I heard you muttering last night."

"Oh, you've made me remember now. I had a wonderful dream about Christmas with my family, but there was something else. What was it?"

The harder Izzy tried to remember, the more it slipped away.

Just then there was a knock on the door.

"Can I come in?" called Princess Ornella.

"Yes," said Izzy, going to the door.

Orlando jumped off the bed and ran to greet Ornella, the bells around his neck tinkling merrily.

"CAT BELLS!" shouted Izzy, making them all jump. "Cat Bells. That was it!"

"What was it?" said Agnes, looking puzzled.

"I had to remember Cat Bells."

"What in the world are you talking about, Izzy?" said Ornella.

"Last night I had a dream and I had to remember Cat Bells, but I can't remember the rest."

"I heard you say 'night, night, Nanny Ellen'," said Agnes.

"That's it," said Izzy, jumping up and down. "My nan told me to go to the dwarfs at Cat Bells. We've all got to go there."

"The only place I know by that name is a small fell in the Lake District near Keswick," said Ornella. "Only we call it 'Cat Belde' or 'den of the wild cat.' It's the home of King Gregorian of the Derwentwater Dwarfs."

"That must be it, I'm sure Nan is telling us to go there."

"Come, we'll tell my father at once. We've just time before the meeting starts. Izzy, you might have saved months of trial and error to find the place where the spheres are being made."

They hurried along the corridor and found Gillie talking with Lord Goshawk. They were laughing and chatting like old friends. Agnes scowled at both of them.

"Where's the lovely Agnes today?" said Gavin, looking around as though he couldn't see her. "And will someone introduce me to this young warrior?"

He winked at Gillie, who put a hand over his mouth to stifle a laugh.

Agnes was in danger of boiling over.

"This is how I normally dress," she spluttered. "If you don't like it, you know what you can do. And I thought *you* were my friend," she said, glaring at Gillie.

"Come," said Ornella. "No more teasing, please. We'll be late if we don't go now."

The meeting place was in one of the Ceremonial Towers and was just as grand as the banquet hall. Benches were set out in semicircles to face a raised dais, upon which stood three chairs.

On the left of the hall a large seagull stood, preening himself in a holding pen. The room was packed with the great lords and ladies who had been at the banquet. The chamber buzzed with noise and excitement.

"This way," said Ornella. She led them to the front and bade them sit on the benches to the right.

"When the king enters you must stand and wait until he is seated before you sit," she said. "I must go to see him with your news now, Izzy."

Ornella quickly strode across to a door set in a wood-panelled wall behind the dais, and disappeared inside.

Three small fairies were sitting in front of Izzy. They looked out of place amongst the grand assembly and one of them was crying.

"Are you all right?" said Izzy. She leaned forward and touched her on the shoulder.

"Yes, thank you, it's just that it's such a relief to be here," said the fairy. "My name's Rose, and this is Lily and Daisy." They nodded to Izzy.

"We're hoping the king can help us. We've had to leave our homes," said Lily.

"That's terrible," said Izzy. "I'm sure the king will be able to think of something to help."

A few minutes later Seraphino Cosmos swept in. He

was dressed in a black suit and cloak. As he moved, the cloak swirled, revealing bright jewel colours depicting the planets. He took his seat on the dais.

Just as the heralds entered Ornella reappeared. She took her place next to the chancellor and nodded to Izzy.

Suddenly there was a fanfare of trumpets.

"Lords, ladies, councillors and guests, please be upstanding for His Majesty King Thodrek," cried one of the heralds.

Izzy rose with the rest of the assembly. The atmosphere was tense and tinged with anticipation, perhaps she, too, would get some answers.

12

The Meeting

King Thodrek entered and a hush descended on the chamber. When the king and the whole assembly were seated, Seraphino Cosmos came forward to address the meeting.

"Lords, ladies, councillors and guests, this meeting has been called because of the disturbing events regarding the tooth crisis. We also have a seagull representative present, because of an unprovoked attack on Princess Ornella yesterday."

There was a gasp of horror from the assembly.

"To continue … you will see the exhibit in the glass case, proof of how the teeth are being taken. Also, among our guests we have three flower fairies. They will give evidence of the damage being done to the environment due to the fading magic. And we must also welcome a human child, Izzy Green." He indicated to where Izzy was seated.

Another gasp came from the assembly and a murmur ran through the hall – *The Child of Light! Is it her?*

"The first matter on the agenda is the flower fairies," continued the chancellor.

The three small fairies sitting in front of Izzy went up on to the raised platform.

Rose was the first to speak.

"We've had to leave our homes because of the pollution, everyone is using more and more pesticides and it's choking us."

"But the humans only started using more pesticides

because we weren't invisible anymore and couldn't work in their gardens," continued Lily.

"We met some Landwihta on the way here," said Daisy, "and they can't work in the fields and orchards any more either. Without invisibility they would be turned to dust for certain if they stayed."

A buzz of voices came from the assembly and the king raised his hand for quiet.

"Continue if you please," he said to the fairies.

"The Cofgodas are suffering too," said Daisy. "And the humans are upset because things keep going missing, while ants, mice and spiders are creeping back into their houses, whenever they can."

"Landwihta? Cofgodas?" whispered Izzy.

"Land spirits and house elves," said Agnes. "People don't realise, we live alongside humans everywhere, helping out with almost everything. Without us, crops fail and pests thrive. House elves are most at risk because they live inside human homes."

The king came forward and called for questions from the assembly. The fairies answered as best as they could and then returned to their seats.

The chancellor stepped forward again. "We now come to the matter of the seagulls mobbing Her Highness." He turned to the large bird that was waiting in the pen. "What have you to say?"

"We were totally in the right," said the gull. "The princess was in our air space."

"I'm sorry," said the king leaning forward, "what do you mean *your* air space?"

"That's what I said, "our air space". It's bought and paid for. No one can enter without our permission. It runs from one end of the island to the other."

"How exactly did you pay for this privilege, and who

sold you the rights?" said the king.

"The Company of St Onomans sold it to us," said the bird.

The king could hardly be heard above the pandemonium that broke out, and Izzy almost fell off her chair. "That's my dad's company," she hissed to Agnes.

"How can a company sell you rights to air space?" the king shouted.

The seagull shifted uneasily from one webbed foot to the other. "We haven't done anything wrong," he said. "We paid good money. Well, not exactly money. We promised to tell the company anything of interest that happens in this area."

"You mean you *spy?*" said the king.

"No. We're 'information consultants'. It's all above board – we've got a contract."

"I think not," said King Thodrek. "Didn't your leader consider how this 'Company' could sell you something that is free?"

"We're just following orders," replied the bird, looking extremely uncomfortable. "The company said if we didn't do as we were told they'd stop us flying."

"Tell your leader to make an appointment to see me," said the king, going red in the face. "I believe he has been seriously misled."

The bird nodded, waddled out of the pen and was ushered out of the hall by two guards less than half its size.

Seraphino Cosmos stood again and held up his hand for silence. "We now come to the matter of the missing teeth. The king will address you on the gravity of the situation."

The king came to the front of the platform. He motioned for the sphere to be brought to him, and then held it aloft with both arms.

"We have not been able to find a way to open this as yet, but from the information Orlando has given us we know the sphere contains at least one tooth … that of Izzy Green."

"Oh, my tooth," cried Izzy, jumping up.

She immediately sat down again feeling silly.

"Come here, child," said the king in a kindly tone. "Don't be afraid. Look, you can hold the sphere if you wish."

Izzy stood up reluctantly. There was an eerie silence and she knew the entire assembly was watching her. She walked towards the king. The sphere wasn't quite like she remembered, it was much bigger, the size of a large beach ball. Then she realised, it was her that was smaller. She held out her arms and took it from the king. It was cold and smooth, no join could be seen anywhere. As she turned it over she felt a tingling sensation in her hands. A trapdoor opened on one side and two mechanical arms dropped out, limp and lifeless, along with a few dozen milk teeth. There was a gasp from everyone, including the king.

"Well, Izzy, you've proved your worth already. Not one of our advisors has been able to work out how to open it."

"But I didn't do anything," said Izzy.

The king beamed at her. "The greatest power is often the most subtle, my child. There's enough magic in those few teeth to sustain us for at least a month. Now go and take your place again with Agnes. I hope you will not mind if we keep your tooth. We will of course make sure you have the usual payment of a wonderful dream."

Izzy curtsied to the king and returned to her seat, still confused, but pleased to be out of view and back in the crowd once more.

The king addressed the assembly again. "This is a grave matter. We need to find out who is taking the teeth and why. Our advisors have confirmed this sphere is definitely of dwarfish manufacture. And now thanks to the Child of Light, we think probably the Derwentwater Dwarfs."

The king stopped as Seraphino Cosmos made a sudden movement. The chancellor looked startled and uneasy.

"Chancellor, are you all right?" asked the king.

"Yes. Yes thank you, Your Majesty. I … I wasn't aware we knew the source for the manufacture of the spheres."

The king continued, "I know there are some among you who suspect the goblins but I will not tolerate Goblinist prejudice. Proof must be obtained before any rash action is taken. I put it to the vote that an expedition be raised to approach the Derwentwater Dwarfs to confirm the origins of the silver sphere. All those in favour?"

There was a general *Aye,* from the assembly.

"All those against?"

There was silence.

"Very well. The motion is carried. I have given a great deal of thought as to who should go on this mission. I believe Izzy Green has been sent to us for this very purpose. Gilbert Golden Oak, Agnes Ash and Orlando are also to go, under the protection of Lord Falcon. There are several coincidences in the coming together of this group that should not be ignored."

An elven lord stood up. "Your Majesty, this Gilbert Golden Oak and Agnes Ash, they are just wood elves are they not?"

"I can think of no one better for this mission. Both Gilbert and Agnes have proved their courage beyond question. It is one thing to be brave when one has been trained to fight, but quite another to show such courage when one has not."

"Oh, Izzy, a chance to prove I'm a real warrior at last," whispered Agnes, her eyes shining.

"I'm really pleased for you, Agnes, but hopefully there won't be any more fighting," Izzy whispered back.

Gavin stood up suddenly. "Your Majesty, may I be included on the mission?"

"Yes," said the king, "I think that is a very good idea."

"Well I don't think so," said Agnes in a loud whisper. She turned around and glared at Gavin. "I'm sorry, but I think it might be dangerous taking someone who is obviously so hasty."

"That's a bit rich coming from you," said Gavin, laughing and rubbing his nose.

Agnes turned to face the front again, and Izzy could see she was furious.

The king looked around the assembly and seemed satisfied that there were no further comments or questions. "And now, Chancellor, if you would be so kind, please close the meeting."

The chancellor did as he was bid and everyone filed out.

Ornella took them back to her day chamber and ordered lunch. They were all starving and everyone ate in silence, until Izzy suddenly remembered something that had bothered her during the meeting.

"Ornella, the company the seagull mentioned, it's my father's company."

"Are you sure?" said Ornella. "Goblins are sure to be behind that too, then."

"You're a Goblinist?" blurted out Gillie in surprise.

Ornella glared at him then regained her composure. "I have my reasons."

"But how could it be goblins?" argued Gillie. "How

could they run a human company completely in secret? They'd be turned to dust … it's ridiculous. We need to talk to the dwarfs first and get the facts straight, not jump to conclusions."

Ornella didn't answer, but sat smoothing Orlando who was curled up on her lap.

"What about the air space then?" said Agnes. "It proves this company is up to no good."

"I don't think you can say it proves anything," said Gillie. "Simply that the company has ambitions. Perhaps air space *can* be bought."

"But it can't be right to charge for air," said Izzy, giving Orlando a hard look as he purred contentedly.

There was a knock on the door and King Thodrek entered with Gavin.

"Father, I'm glad you're here. There is something you need to know. Izzy's father works for a company called St Onomans."

"That is a strange coincidence indeed," said the king. "We will have to be extra careful in any dealings we might have with this company, for Izzy's sake."

"I've just remembered something," said Gillie. "Some swifts we met on the way here told us the spheres were flying out of London. I'm not sure it can be the Derwentwater Dwarfs after all."

"Well, they could be making them for someone else. Let us not speculate any further. We must start by visiting the dwarfs," said the king.

"I agree," said Ornella. "*Everyone* has been jumping to conclusions. I will get to the bottom of this with the dwarfs."

"Oh no," said King Thodrek. "You're not going anywhere, Ornella. You were lucky you weren't seriously injured yesterday."

"Father, I really must insist …"

"I know what you're going to say, Ornella, and the answer is still 'no'. Come to see me later. I have a more important mission for you."

"But, Father …"

"Goodnight, to you all," said the king, raising his voice slightly and moving towards the door.

They all bowed and Izzy curtsied as the king left them.

Ornella told them all to rest for the remainder of the day, but it was almost impossible for Izzy. Thoughts plagued her constantly … was her father's company somehow involved in all this? She kept thinking about the meeting in the penthouse and that creepy harsh voice. The voyage to the dwarfs would begin tomorrow, but for Izzy tomorrow couldn't come soon enough.

13

The Voyage

In the morning Izzy went down to the bay where the ship was moored. She gasped; it was the most beautiful vessel she had ever seen. It had a sleek white hull with gold rails, and three tall masts that rose out of the deck, which carried white furled sails. Elves hurried past with provisions which they carried down to the end of the pier, like ants, scrambling backwards and forwards onto the ship in a constant chain.

Gillie rushed past with a large bundle of stores. "Hi, Izzy, are you looking forward to the voyage?"

"Yes. Are you sure you can you manage, Gillie?"

"Yes, yes, I'm fine," yelled Gillie as he tottered up the gangplank. "Where do you want these, Lord Falcon?"

"Put them over by the rail please, Gillie."

Gillie turned but tripped on his bootlace. He stumbled and the stores went flying. Izzy watched a box arc through the air as if in slow motion. It gave Gavin a glancing blow on the head, knocking him overboard.

"GAVIN," screamed Agnes, who was working nearby. Dropping what she was doing, she leapt onto the rail. The next moment she dived into the sea. Everyone rushed to the side of the ship.

Izzy held her breath and searched the waters desperately. There was no trace of either of them. She looked at Lord Falcon, then at Gillie.

He was staring down into the sea and wringing his hands together. "Oh, I'm sorry. I'm so sorry. What have I done? I'm so clumsy."

Izzy took his hand to calm him, but her own heart was racing. "It was an accident. You didn't mean it. Don't worry, I'm sure everything will be all right."

Minutes were passing and there was still no sign.

"Look," shouted Lord Falcon.

A few bubbles broke the surface, then Agnes burst through, gasping for breath. She held Gavin's head above the waves. He looked unconscious. Then she swam for the dock, one arm around Gavin, the other pulling as hard as she could.

"You elves on the shore," called Lord Falcon, "help Agnes."

The elves jumped in and helped to haul the pair out of the water. Agnes stood exhausted, unable to take her eyes off Gavin while the elves worked to revive him.

Izzy and Gillie ran to join her.

"Gavin, please be all right. I'm so sorry," said Gillie.

Gavin choked and spluttered back to life. "Ouch, my head." He struggled to sit up. "What happened?"

"Gillie happened," snapped Agnes, glaring at Gillie.

"It was an accident, Agnes," said Izzy.

"I think it's time he learned to swim," said Agnes. "It could be him that gets pushed overboard next."

She took Gillie by the hand and marched him off to the shallows, where she promptly pushed him in.

When the ship was finally provisioned and ready to sail, Izzy stood between Gillie and Agnes on the pier that ran out from the rocky promontory at the end of the bay. Gavin had recovered, Gillie had learned how to swim, and strangely, Agnes was cross with both of them.

A fanfare sounded and Izzy watched the royal party making their way down from the palace; it looked like the whole court was coming to see them off.

They stood waiting to say their goodbyes to Ornella

and the king.

"I wish you were coming with us," said Izzy, "we'll really miss you."

"I know how disappointed you must be to miss out on an adventure," said Agnes.

"Won't the king change his mind?" asked Gillie.

"We would all do our best to protect you," said Gavin, with a bow.

"It's for the best," said Ornella. "My father has another important task for me. I will see you all again soon, I hope."

The king came forward, and they said goodbye and thanked him for everything. Agnes was very pleased with her new bow and arrows. Gillie had a sword from the armoury, although he looked as if he didn't know what to do with it, and Gavin had stocked up on arrows. In place of a weapon, Izzy had been given a small whistle, which could be used to summon basking sharks, and everyone wore a new cloak for camouflage and warmth.

"Time to go," said Lord Falcon. "Goodbye, Your Majesty, Princess Ornella. I will send word as soon as we have landed. Have you the king's letter for the dwarfs, Gillie?"

"Yes, Lord Falcon," said Gillie, patting his chest pocket.

They boarded the sailing ship, and under Lord Falcon's guidance it moved out past the safety of the bay and into the open sea. They all stood at the stern and waved as the shore fell away into the distance. It was a beautiful morning with not a cloud in sight. The sun sparkled on the sea and dazzled their eyes. Izzy took Orlando below and he curled up on her bunk bed.

"You'd sleep all day *and* night, wouldn't you?" she said laughing at him. "It is a shame Ornella's not coming, but I was getting worried the way you were flirting so outrageously with her."

"Don't worry, Izzy, no one could take your place. I am a cat though, and a charming one at that," he grinned.

"You're impossible," she said, but gave him a long smooth nonetheless.

When Izzy went back up on deck she found Gillie and Agnes looking over the side, fascinated by the spray and foam. Small fish were swimming alongside, jumping and playing in the waves.

Lord Falcon was at the helm and he called them around. "If you're excited by those tiny fish, perhaps it's time we harnessed something larger."

He took the small whistle around his neck, and blew two low, almost silent, notes. Before long a basking shark appeared. He threw lines out over the bow and engaged its help to tow the ship. Izzy grabbed the rail as the ship suddenly accelerated and skimmed across the waves. It seemed as though the elves could achieve anything with the help of nature.

"Where are we headed, Lord Falcon?"

"We're going to be sailing up the west coast as far as St Bees Head, where there's a long sandy beach where we can land. It's near the Lake District, one of the most beautiful places in Britain."

"I've never been there," said Izzy. "It sounds amazing."

The rest of the day passed without incident. The fine weather continued with a light breeze and they made good time. After lunch, which they took on deck, Lord Falcon let them all have a turn at steering the ship.

Gavin had felt queasy as soon as they'd left the shelter of the bay, but now joined them. He was looking much less green. Agnes fussed over him, which certainly improved his spirits.

"You two seem to be getting on well now," whispered Gillie.

"I'd do exactly the same for you if you were ill," said Agnes, but she did smile all the same.

"Look, what's that?" called Izzy, pointing up to a spot in the sky behind them.

Gillie tried to see what she was looking at. "Where?"

"It's gone now, but I was sure I saw a bird, following us."

"Never mind that, Izzy, I think it's my turn to steer again. I'm looking forward to it. Lord Falcon taught me all about the wind and the sails. Port and starboard too … that's left and right in nautical terms, you know."

Izzy laughed. "You've really taken to sailing haven't you?"

"I know. It's great isn't it?" Gillie scampered off to join Lord Falcon at the wheel.

Izzy turned quickly and looked up again. Yes, there. Just a dot, but she was sure there was something, perhaps a seagull, spying on them. She made a mental note to keep watch.

14

Nixies

The weather was not so good when they got up the next day. There were gusty squalls and the sea was choppy. They rounded Lands End in the early morning and started sailing up the west coast.

It was nightfall before they reached the Menai Straits, not a good time to negotiate the narrow waters. Lord Falcon called them all together and gave instructions about using the safety lines. He made sure they were all wearing life jackets, but told them to stay below as much as possible.

Izzy tossed and turned in her bunk. She felt restless, but didn't want to wake Orlando curled up by her feet, so she went on deck to find Lord Falcon.

"Hello, Izzy, can't sleep?" He pulled on the wheel and guided the ship into the middle of the channel.

"No. Is it all right if I stay up here with you for a bit?"

Lord Falcon nodded, and Izzy wrapped her cloak around herself for warmth.

She stood lost in thought for a moment or two, watching him expertly manoeuvre the ship through the swirling waters. The fresh wind blew into her face, making her feel even more wide-awake.

"Lord Falcon. Why do elves get turned into dust?"

"My, you have been thinking," said Lord Falcon, laughing. "Well, Izzy, there are three forms of existence; matter, energy, and a third state. Your scientists know of this as the 'quantum state'. It is on this level that all magical creatures exist; it's neither matter nor energy. The simplest way I can explain – it is a state of possibilities."

"I think I've heard about that, Lord Falcon." Izzy frowned.

"Our magic is the ability to manipulate both energy and matter," he continued. "And that is why the source of all power is children's teeth, for children see the world without constraints, a world where anything is possible."

"But that still doesn't explain why you get turned to dust."

"It's because the quantum level is just possibility, we both exist and do not exist at the same moment. But when we are seen, one of those possibilities must be realised. If you do not believe in magic, that belief *becomes* our reality and we are transformed to nothing more than simple atoms … dust."

"So, you have to believe you will see an elf, in order to *see* an elf."

"Yes, I know, it sounds like a paradox. Some humans have given themselves quite a headache trying to understand it, especially someone called Einstein, I heard," he said smiling.

Just then, Gillie staggered up on deck and lurched towards them.

"It's getting really rough," he shouted.

"Come over here and hold onto the lines," ordered Lord Falcon. "We don't want to lose you overboard, Gillie, even though you can swim now."

Izzy reached out her hand to Gillie and helped secure him.

"Thanks, Izzy. I'm okay now," said Gillie.

They both fell silent. Lord Falcon needed all his wits and energy to manoeuvre through the dangerous waters. The ship raced through the entrance to the straits and under the first bridge. Then the water started to get really rough, swirling, and crashing over the rocks.

"Don't worry, it's just the Swellies. I've sailed them many times, there's nothing to worry about," shouted Lord Falcon.

Suddenly the lines went slack and the ship spun and lurched precariously to one side. It seemed like the basking shark was no longer towing them.

Lord Falcon fought with the wheel to bring the ship under control again. "Izzy, Gillie, I need you to look out for the rocks. We've just lost our power."

"What's happened?" cried Izzy as she clung on to the rails. She strained her eyes in the darkness to see.

"I don't know," shouted Lord Falcon. "It seems like the lines have broken."

Izzy and Gillie called directions to Lord Falcon as best they could.

As they passed under the second bridge, the worst seemed to be over. The end of the strait was in sight now. Izzy started to relax and heaved a huge sigh of relief as the water became less choppy.

But then a cry sounded out, barely audible above the noise of the wind … like the screeching tyres of a car.

"Listen," said Izzy, "I thought I heard screaming coming from the water."

"I don't hear anything," said Lord Falcon. "Are you sure?"

"Yes, listen," said Gillie, "I hear it too."

"There it is again," said Izzy. "It sounds unearthly."

"Oh my ears," cried Gillie, falling to the deck holding his head in agony.

"Oh no." Lord Falcon's face clouded as he, too, heard the cries. "Go rouse Agnes and Gavin. It's Nixies."

"What are Nixies?" yelled Izzy.

"Go, Izzy. GET THE OTHERS."

74

As Izzy turned to go, Gavin appeared on deck, sword in hand, and Agnes was close behind with her stave, ready to fight.

"What's going on?" shouted Gavin.

"Water demons, I think," called Gillie.

Izzy cannoned past them, desperate to get to Orlando.

He looked up as she ran into the cabin. "What's that dreadful …? MEOW OW," he yelled, and disappeared back under the bedclothes.

"We're being attacked." She grabbed his middle and pulled. "*Claws,* Orlando. LET GO!"

"NO. I'd rather stay here."

"Get in my backpack and keep out of sight," ordered Izzy. She slung the backpack across her shoulders and raced back up on deck just as the Nixies' screeching chant rose in a crescendo. Helpless against the horrific noise, she staggered, dazed and confused.

Agnes sank to her knees, head buried in her cloak, cursing audibly for being so weak. Gavin and Gillie valiantly tried to remain upright, ready to fight. But the cacophony grew worse, rising and falling in an unholy choral symphony.

Unable to bear it any longer, Gavin and Gillie collapsed, rocking backwards and forwards in pain. Now only Lord Falcon remained standing, struggling to keep the ship on course.

The Nixies came over the rail and poured onto the deck like a tide of living seaweed. Izzy trembled as the blue, scaly creatures scuttled towards them, sideling like crabs, green straggling hair hanging across their hideous faces.

Lord Falcon drew his wand, but was unable to form the ancient words because the ghastly wailing numbed his brain. Wresting the useless wand from his hand, the Nixies surrounded him and he too succumbed to the inevitable.

The fight lost, the ship theirs – the Nixies steered towards the shore and ran it aground.

Izzy lay helpless, terrified, waiting to discover their fate. Then the rain started. Cold and penetrating, it fell in great sheets, soaking them through to the bone. Izzy looked up at tall figures in hooded cloaks that loomed through the mist. Like ghosts they glided, surrounding them. Izzy wanted to hide, she wanted to close her eyes, but was irresistibly drawn to look at them. As the figures moved closer their features became visible, no longer obscured by the shadows of their heavy shrouds. They wore silver grey armour, their faces beautiful. Yet somehow, they managed to instil more terror than the hideous Nixies.

"I think I preferred the Nixies," shouted Gillie, still holding his ears.

The newcomers quickly shot a dart at each of the male members of the party while they were still paralysed by the Nixies" screeching. The darts disintegrated as soon as they pierced the skin, in a puff of black dust.

"Elf shot," gasped Lord Falcon. "It's the Dokkalfar …"

The Nixies became silent at once and slid back into the sea, their job done.

As the darts took effect, Izzy and Agnes could only watch as their friends bent over in terrible pain. Their new captors herded them off the ship and onto the shores of Anglesey.

"What have you done?" cried Izzy in alarm. "Will the arrows kill them?"

"The malady will pass," said the leader. "But the darts make it easier to handle all of you, until you are secured."

"You mean imprisoned," said Agnes hotly.

The leader pushed Agnes forward roughly. "MOVE GIRL, I have no need to talk to you."

The group was led along a coastal path while the rain continued to sleet down on them. Izzy struggled to see anything in the enclosing gloom. The sound of marching feet on the shingle, the smell of wet sea grass, the calls of birds in the distance and the howling wind, overwhelmed her senses. She wanted to escape. Perhaps there was a chance in the darkness, but what would she do? Where would she go? She wavered, unable to think straight, and before she knew it the group came to a halt, the opportunity lost. They stood in front of a grassy bank, but there was nothing to be seen except a low mound covered in mud.

The Dokkalfar leader started to chant in a strange language. He pulled off his hood to reveal shoulder length, white hair and a silver circlet upon his brow, which began to glow. The light, dim at first, gradually pierced the gloom in an ethereal jade light, and outlined an arched doorway which was decorated in runes. A beam shot from the centre of the circlet and played on the symbols. As it did so, they too, started to emit the same eerie glow. Slowly, a door appeared in the bank, then opened to reveal steps leading down.

Izzy clasped Agnes' hand. "What's going to happen to us? What do they want?" she gasped. "Will I ever see my parents again?"

"Stay close to me, Izzy. I'm sure we'll make it out of this."

Izzy wished she felt as confident as Agnes sounded. Her heart was pounding and she felt sick, as well as being wet and miserable. As the doors slid shut behind them and darkness closed in all around, she wondered if Agnes still felt the same.

15

The Dokkalfar

They went down the steps, and into the darkness of the tunnel. There wasn't much light, but the Dokkalfar seemed to be able to see. On and on they went, first left, then right, going steadily down the whole time. The air became difficult to breathe and the walls ran with moisture. Then they started to climb and the air got better, but it was still cold and damp.

Izzy tried to take note of the different twists and turns, but there were too many. Suddenly the tunnel opened out into a large chamber. She could feel it more than see it, because of a change in the air. She heard the sound of many elves murmuring and the rustle of garments.

They were led into the centre of the cavern. Izzy could just make out a raised stone platform with a stone chair. A purple and gold rug was draped over it. On this sat one of the Dokkalfar. He shared the same mean eyes and same lean body shape of their captor. On either side of him crouched two Nixies, like pet dogs.

Gradually the darkness seemed to lift as her eyes adjusted. The cavern was immense. Light reflected off a subterranean pool that stretched away into the gloom. Izzy shivered, it didn't look at all inviting.

"Who among you speaks for you?" barked the Dokkalfar on the stone chair. His voice was harsh and cruel.

Nobody answered.

"Which of you is leader?" he commanded.

Lord Falcon staggered forward, clutching his stomach.

"I am the leader – Lord Falcon, of the Ljosalfar. And if I am correct, you must be King of the Dokkalfar?"

"I ask the questions in my realm. You invaded our straits without paying the toll and must now face the consequences."

"I have sailed these waters for many years. These straits are free for all to come and go."

"Not any longer, Ljosalfar, we have purchased the rights from St Onomans."

Izzy let out a gasp.

The king leaned forward and scanned the group, his eyes coming to rest on Izzy. "Bring that female forward. Let me look at her."

Izzy was pushed to her knees before the king. "You're a child, a human child. What are you doing in the company of elves?"

Before she could answer, Agnes rushed forward and landed a blow on the king's shoulder with her stick. "Leave her alone," she shouted.

Six darts thudded into Agnes and she collapsed on her knees in agony.

"Why does this warrior still have weapons?" bellowed the king, rubbing his shoulder. "Someone will pay for this."

The leader of their guards stepped forward and lifted Agnes by the arms. "My Lord, I did not expect a female to give any trouble."

"Elander, you always were soft hearted like your mother. You must learn there is no place for sentiment in our world, brother."

The king took out a black ebony wand from his cloak, and lightning shot from the end, hitting Elander in the chest. He gasped and dropped Agnes.

Everyone watched in horror as Elander stood transfixed in pain. The king gave a flick of his wrist, and once released, Elander crashed to the floor.

As Izzy cradled Agnes, she saw the hatred in Elander's eyes and almost felt sorry for him, but surely someone that looked so cold couldn't be soft hearted?

The king motioned to Elander to get up. "Take the prisoners to the cells and send a message for their ransom. And try not to mess it up." He turned to the Nixies. "You may go. You have done well."

The Nixies scuttled off sideways and slid into the uninviting waters of the subterranean lake.

The effects of the poison darts were beginning to wear off the others, but Agnes was still crippled with pain. Gavin and Gillie both hurried to carry her. She looked extremely ill and could barely stand.

"I've got her, I've got her," cried Gavin. "Take her pack, Gillie."

They followed Elander, who led them out of the hall and back into the tunnels. As soon as the main chamber was out of sight, Elander suddenly turned and approached Izzy briskly. She was filled with trepidation.

"Here, take this for the female." He pulled a small pouch out from inside his armour and thrust it into her hand.

"What is it?" she asked, her hand trembling.

"It's a sleeping draught, it will help the pain … one spoonful for pain, two for sleep. Your friend has great valour and should not be punished further. But I warn you, say nothing of this to anyone."

"Thank you," whispered Izzy. She nervously stuffed the potion into her coat pocket. Perhaps she had misjudged him after all.

They followed in silence down to another level where there were holding cells. They were crowded all together into a single large room, just a basic cell carved out of the solid rock. A door constructed from iron bars as thick as an arm covered the entrance, and the only illumination was the dim light that filtered in from what appeared to be glow-worms, captured inside globes hanging in the tunnel. All their weapons and possessions, including Lord Falcon's wand, were taken and stashed in a side room further down the tunnel.

Elander gave orders for food and water to be brought to the prisoners. When the guards had gone, Lord Falcon seized the chance to speak with him.

"Elander, we are kindred; the action of your king threatens to bring war between our peoples. Even though a schism occurred years ago, we should not fight each other. There are enough foes in this world to fight with better reason, and certainly not for money."

"I cannot discuss this with you, it is too dangerous." Elander turned to go.

"Wait. Isn't peace worth the risk? Think of the benefits to be gained from friendship."

Elander paused, deep in thought, considering Lord Falcon's words, the stress clearly visible on his face. "While Ragnestar remains king, he must be obeyed. By his command, mercy and kindness is a weakness. And I have already been far too weak."

"Please," said Izzy, coming to the bars, "you've helped Agnes already. That took courage, not weakness. And you shouldn't trust St Onomans. Won't you help us?"

Elander's face became calm, and he smiled for the first time. He took a small step towards Izzy and looked closely at her. "You are wise, little one, for a human. You're right I do not trust that company, they want us to give them information, and perhaps more. Since my brother has been dealing with them his rule has become cruel. And he has the power and wealth to enforce it. For the future of my own people, and for you, I … I want to help."

"Join with us then," said Lord Falcon. "You must have elves that are loyal to you. Free us."

There was a sound from further down the corridor. Elander looked away from Izzy and took a step back. His expression became stern and tortured once again.

"*Enough.* I have done more than I should already. My life would be forfeit if I freed you."

He turned and walked away just as the food and water arrived.

There wasn't time to dwell on the missed opportunity and Agnes was still bent over with the pain. Izzy quickly took the jug and poured some water into a cup. There was a small spoon inside the pouch, and she put one measure into the cup and stirred it well.

Agnes leaned on one elbow and drank, slowly at first, and then as she started to get her colour back, she quickly finished it. Gavin and Gillie looked on anxiously.

"Oh, that feels better," exclaimed Agnes, managing a small smile. "Thank you, Izzy – all of you for looking after me."

"I'm glad you're feeling better, my dear," said Lord Falcon. "If only we could have persuaded Elander to set us free. He seemed to change when you spoke to him, Izzy."

"I don't think I said anything special, just the truth."

"Yes," said Lord Falcon. "But telling the truth, and getting someone to believe it, are two very different things. And he believed you."

16

A Light in the Darkness

There was nothing to do now but wait. Trapped below ground in a dank, dark dungeon and with no hope of rescue, Izzy felt defeated. She went over to sit with Agnes.

"Cheer up," said Agnes. "That Elander might change his mind."

"I don't think so. Why should he risk his life for us?"

Izzy felt a movement in her backpack. It was Orlando stretching. "Orlando, I'd forgotten about you with all the excitement." She reached into the backpack and pulled him out, hugging him close while tears ran down her cheeks.

Orlando purred happily for a moment as Izzy smoothed him, then he looked around. "I say, where are we? Is it safe to come out? This doesn't look too nice a place."

"You're not kidding," said Izzy, choking back the tears and managing a small laugh. "Oh, Orlando, there's such a lot to tell you. You haven't been asleep all the time, have you?"

"What, with all that wailing going on? Impossible. I wrapped my tail around my ears, stuck my head in your jumper and waited for it to stop … then, maybe, I did have a quick nap."

Lord Falcon studied Orlando quietly for a moment. "I think I have a plan. Orlando, do you think you can squeeze through the bars? If you can get to the chamber where our things are and get my wand I'll be able to free us."

"Consider it done," said Orlando with a wide grin.

"Please be careful," warned Izzy as she put him down.

Orlando slid gracefully between the bars and ran silently along the tunnel.

"Where do we go once we get out of this cell?" asked Gavin.

"Good question," said Lord Falcon. "Anyone remember the way back to the top?"

"I tried to keep track," said Izzy, "but there were too many twists and turns, I lost count. And how would we get the door in the side of the hill open? They used runes and a strange language."

"It's similar to our ancient tongue," said Lord Falcon, "but I didn't catch it all."

"What about the lake? That's just above us," said Gillie. "It must come out in the straits. The Nixies slid back into the water after the meeting."

"We don't know how far, or how much of it, is underwater?" said Gavin. "Those creatures must be able to hold their breath a lot longer than us."

"We could climb to the top of the cavern and find a way out," said Izzy. "I'm not going without Orlando, and he doesn't like water."

"First things first," said Lord Falcon. "Let's just get out of this cell."

Orlando ran back along the tunnel with the wand clamped between his teeth. He dropped it just outside the bars, and Lord Falcon reached through and picked it up.

"Well done, Orlando," said Izzy.

Lord Falcon then spoke quietly but clearly in the ancient tongue of the Ljosalfar. From the tip of the wand a bluish grey mist appeared and swirled around the lock on the door. It gave a soft hiss and swung open. "How do you feel, Agnes? Are you fit to walk?"

"I'm more than ready to leave this place – even if I have to crawl."

Gavin and Gillie both looked at her with admiration.

They all made their way along the tunnel until they reached the chamber where their belongings and weapons were stowed. Once they had everything safe about them, they followed Lord Falcon back along the dimly lit passage.

The five of them crept along slowly, trying not to make a sound, Orlando followed behind Izzy, stretching his legs out as he walked. Finally they reached the entrance to the chamber with the stone chair.

Lord Falcon stopped and listened. "I can't hear anything. Let's hope our luck holds." He motioned for them to stay put, and went on ahead to check out the cavern.

Izzy waited anxiously, desperate to get out of this place.

Lord Falcon hurried back. "Come, quickly, it looks as though they've all gone back to their cells, or whatever passes for their accommodation."

As Izzy crowded into the cavern with the others, she saw the lake and shuddered. "I do hope we don't have to swim," she whispered.

"I agree. I don't know what I was thinking even suggesting it," said Gillie.

"Everyone, make your way around the edge," commanded Lord Falcon. "Look for a path leading up or any breeze or draft that might indicate an opening."

They started to clamber over the wet, slippery rocks, the slimy, cold surfaces making every step an ordeal. As they got further from the meeting place, the light got fainter and fainter until there was almost complete darkness.

Izzy slipped, unable to see, she thrust out her hands in desperation. Her forearm caught the side of a large boulder, and she gritted her teeth, trying not to scream.

"What's happened?" whispered Lord Falcon, turning back.

There were frantic whispers as Izzy lay on ground, holding her arm, curled up in pain. "It's ... all right, it's just my arm, I'm all right."

Lord Falcon carefully made his way back to Izzy and examined her arm. "Nothing broken, thank Freya. This is ridiculous, we can barely see a pace ahead, how are we ever going to find a way out?"

Izzy rolled over to get up, but stopped and lay on her back staring into the gloom above them. "Look, up there," she whispered. "I can see a light."

Sure enough a faint glow, far in the distance, broke the darkness.

"It's not an opening, it's moving." said Lord Falcon.

"Dokkalfar," said Gillie. "Let's turn back."

"No, wait," said Izzy. "I think it's a good sign. Let's go on."

"We will trust in Freya and your judgement, Izzy," said Lord Falcon. "Everyone, move to the side of the cavern, we need to climb towards that light."

They scrambled over the rocks to the sloping walls, which were steep and dripped with moisture. It seemed safer than walking, and now able to use both hands and feet, they made better progress. It was exhausting, but after an hour of weary climbing, they could see the light more clearly. As they drew closer they could just make out the shape of a person.

"It's Ornella," gasped Izzy. "I knew someone was following the ship."

Within a few minutes they had come within talking distance.

"Follow me," ordered Ornella. "There is a way out, but

it's very narrow, no more than a fissure in the rocks. I had an awful time to find it and the place is crawling with Dokkalfar."

"Why are you here?" said Gillie. "I thought the king didn't want you to come?"

"I told you he had an important mission for me. Besides, I had to keep an eye on you," said Ornella laughing.

The darkness didn't quite cover Gillie's embarrassment.

"But why didn't you tell us sooner?" asked Izzy.

"Sadly, your disappointment was necessary for the ruse. My father fears those close to him will try to take power for themselves, and he didn't want them to know I was coming with you. But we must go on now. Follow me."

After climbing wearily for what seemed an age, they found the fissure and squeezed through. They were out in the night air at last.

Izzy took deep breaths of the sweet rain-washed air. It smelled wonderful after the smelly, mouldy confines of the damp cavern. She could hardly believe they were free. The rain had swept past and the night was bright and clear. Not good conditions for an escape … but this was as good as it was going to get.

"Come," said Lord Falcon. "We must get moving. We're not safe yet."

"The ship's well guarded, we won't be able to retake it," said Ornella. "There's no defence against those darts."

"Then we must head for the sea," said Lord Falcon. "Izzy and I will call for a basking shark. If we're lucky, perhaps two will come to take us all away."

They hurried along the grassy slopes in silence. A path led away from the mounds and down to the beach. The birds tucked up in their nests complained as they ran past. A few crows cawed and flapped, then settled down again for the night. Finally, the group reached the beach and their feet crunched on the fine shingle once more. Try as hard as they might, they couldn't deaden the sound.

"Oh, I hope no-one hears us," said Izzy. "I don't want to go back to that underground dungeon."

"Don't worry," said Orlando. "We've almost made it. I haven't got nine lives for nothing."

Lord Falcon drew out his whistle, and Izzy did the same. They both blew a silent note and waited. Ten agonising minutes passed before they saw a great shape approaching the shoreline.

"One won't be enough to carry us all," cried Agnes.

"I sent Regan off earlier to try to recruit any falcons that might be in the area, just to be on the safe side," said Ornella. "Hopefully he'll be back soon."

Just then they heard the sound of nesting birds being disturbed once again, and the sound of many feet crunching behind them. Elander was coming down onto the beach with about fifty men, all with their bows at the ready.

Gavin positioned himself in front of Agnes. Gillie did the same with Izzy. Ornella unsheathed her sword in readiness. But Lord Falcon signed for them to stand down.

"We're trapped," cried Izzy, picking up Orlando and holding him close. She buried her face in his fur to hide her tears.

But Elander didn't give the order to shoot. Instead he stood and waited. "You have caused me much embarrassment this night. I dare not go back with the news you've escaped."

"We haven't escaped yet," said Lord Falcon. "You could recapture us with ease."

"Perhaps," said Elander. "I see there are two new additions to your group. Where did they spring from?"

Lord Falcon bowed and extended his arm to Ornella. "May I introduce Princess Ornella, daughter of King Thodrek." He motioned towards the cat that was held tightly by Izzy. "And Orlando, a trusted companion."

Ornella stepped forward, her violet eyes flashed scornfully at Elander.

"I will not treat or beg for our release," she said. "I challenge you to single combat, a princess of the Ljosalfar against a prince of the Dokkalfar. If you win, I will come with you as hostage and the others will go free. But if I win, we all go free."

As Elander's hand moved to the hilt of his sword, Izzy rushed forward, still with Orlando in her arms.

"Please, sir, please don't fight Ornella. I know you're not bad, not after what you did for Agnes. If you let us go, I'm sure King Thodrek would help your people."

Lord Falcon stepped towards Izzy and tried to pull her back, but she reached out her hand, strangely unafraid, and touched Elander's arm that gripped the sword. She felt a warm sensation in her stomach, a feeling of calmness, and smiled at him.

Elander released his grip, looked Izzy straight in the eyes, then bowed to her. "You have found my weakness once again, young lady."

"Being good isn't a weakness," said Izzy.

Elander chuckled. "I trust in you, little one. You bring me hope. You bring us all hope." He smiled at Izzy then turned to his men with raised arms. "This is our time; an opportunity to free our people, we must take it now."

He turned back and bowed to Ornella. "Go now, Princess. Make good your escape. These men are loyal to me, and I cannot go back. We will make our way to your

King Thodrek, and throw ourselves on his mercy."

Lord Falcon bowed to Elander then urged the others on. "Only two merlins, Regan and another, have come. Gavin, Gillie, you take the shark. Izzy, go with Ornella. Agnes and I will take the other merlin."

"Where are we headed?" cried Ornella.

"The same as before," shouted Lord Falcon, "on to St Bees Head. Farewell, Elander, and good luck."

"Farewell and good luck to you also. May Freya go with you."

"You hold Freya as your god?" said Lord Falcon in surprise.

"My mother was a Ljosalfar. Old habits die hard," called Elander with a shrug, and the merlins flew up into the night sky.

17

Dancing with Hares

Dawn was breaking when the two merlins reached the long sandy bay near the village of St Bees. Lord Falcon and Agnes alighted first. Then Ornella and Izzy landed, slipping off Regan's back. Orlando scrambled out of Izzy's backpack and started to groom himself right away. The wind was blowing the last of the ragged clouds northwards and it promised to be a fine day.

It had been a long, cold, journey. Izzy was exhausted, not to mention hungry, as were the others. Looking along the beach to the north she could see the rocky promontory of St Bees Head. The red cliffs on the seaward side were layered with bands of orange through to rust, rising sheer out of the water to an amazing height, with green hills rolling away to the rear.

"That's where you're headed, Izzy," said Lord Falcon, "the base of those red sandstone cliffs."

"Aren't you coming with us?"

"No. I must return to King Thodrek as soon as possible to tell him of Elander and news of the Dokkalfar treachery. Princess Ornella is the leader now."

Izzy was sorry that Lord Falcon was leaving, but she set about helping Ornella gather twigs for a fire. Then, together with Agnes, she foraged for seaweed and shellfish for their breakfast.

Every now and then Izzy glanced nervously at the sky. "Are we safe now, Ornella?"

"They have no idea where we are going, but we won't rest until we are as far away from the Dokkalfar as possible. By the way, Izzy, that was very well done, the way you persuaded Elander to let us all go."

"Lord Falcon said that, but I didn't do anything."

"Don't underestimate your powers."

"Powers?"

"Trust me, you have powers." Ornella smiled. "But I can say no more, because you must discover them for yourself."

Izzy was confused. What had she done? What powers? She sat down by the fire, thinking hard, until she noticed Gavin and Gillie arrive on the basking shark. She got up and ran over to greet them.

They waded through the water and struggled up the beach, rubbing their arms to keep warm.

"Mmm, that smells good," said Gavin.

"Ornella's just following the guidelines in the 'Elf Guide Book for Survival'," laughed Izzy.

After they had eaten, everyone looked much better. They tidied the beach and put the fire out, and Lord Falcon prepared to go. Izzy managed a smile and a wave as he climbed onto Ornella's merlin, Regan. He turned and waved back as they took off, graceful as ever.

"May Freya go with you," called Ornella as he disappeared into the morning sky. She turned to the others, "Well, I suppose we should get moving too, before the beach becomes crowded with humans."

Izzy and the rest of the group followed Ornella, walking up the beach towards the red cliffs.

"Come on, Puss," called Izzy, and Orlando came running, tail high in the air.

They soon reached the base of the cliffs and the start of the grasslands. The tall grasses swayed around Izzy, hemming her in and limiting her view. She started to feel seasick with the constant movement.

94

She stared up into the sky. "Are those puffins, Ornella?"

"Yes," said Ornella, "and rare black guillemots nest on the cliff, too."

"Oh, I wish I could see them."

"We have to turn inland and head for Keswick."

"Won't Keswick be full of people?"

"That's what this is for." Ornella reached beneath her bodice and showed Izzy her necklace, which held a shard of tooth, set in a golden clasp.

"Is that my tooth?"

"It is. And more than enough magic for a little invisibility," said Ornella. "Now, Izzy, please take out *your* necklace, and blow three long notes on the whistle."

Izzy was puzzled. "I thought it was just for the basking sharks?"

Ornella laughed. "Just wait and see what you catch."

Izzy put the little silver whistle to her mouth and blew three times. Within a few minutes the ground started to shake.

The vibrations travelled up her body, and she looked at Ornella, fearful of what was coming. Suddenly three hares came thundering out of the long grass. Izzy took a step back and they skidded to a halt in front of her.

She choked as their hot breath engulfed her, and found she was staring straight up a pair of nostrils, attached to a large whiskery head.

"They're as big as a horse," gasped Izzy.

Ornella laughed. "Good thing they don't understand you. You might upset them."

The lead hare twitched his long tawny ears and stared at Izzy with fluid brown eyes.

"Pat him," said Ornella.

Izzy tentatively reached out her hand, and was

surprised at how soft his coat was.

Ornella stepped towards the hare, and he crouched down low so she could climb onto his back. "Give me your hand, Izzy."

Izzy stowed Orlando safely in her backpack and, taking Ornella's hand, climbed up behind her.

Agnes scrambled up onto the second hare and held out her hand to Gillie. "Come on. It can't be any worse than sitting on Orlando."

"They go a lot faster than Orlando," said Ornella. "Be sure to hold on tight."

Gavin swung himself up onto the last hare and nodded that he was ready to go.

After a final check, Ornella leaned forward and whispered in one of the hare's long ears.

Izzy shrieked as it leapt high in the air, then took off through the grass, the others leaping and tearing along beside it.

"This is great," yelled Agnes, a wide grin on her face as they drew alongside.

Izzy didn't answer, she needed all her breath just to hold on tight, but Agnes was right – this was far more exhilarating than flying on the back of a falcon. At every pounding step she could feel the miles hastening away.

The long grass swept back on each side of the hare's body, like waves breaking over the bows of a ship, as it plunged and leapt its way across the terrain. The wind buffeted Izzy's face and her eyes were streaming, but she didn't care.

On and on they went, now racing across meadows, now along flower-filled pathways beside the fields. The hares didn't seem to tire.

The sun came out and Izzy could smell the rich sweet earth and all the wild flowers in the hedgerows.

The landscape was changing now. Small fells and lakes made up the terrain, and when the hares carried them to the top of each hill, the views were amazing.

"Look, you can see scars on the hillside where the dwarfs mined for lead and copper in the past," shouted Ornella. "It shows we're on the right track."

Izzy nodded, but still couldn't speak, her breath jolted out of her by the bucking motion of the animal.

The hares kept up the pace all morning, until at last they began to slow down. They finally stopped on the side of a hill where a small beck ran along the bottom.

Ornella slid down and Izzy jumped off beside her, and the others did the same.

Izzy patted her hare goodbye, and Ornella thanked them. They immediately took off like mad things, leaping and racing each other down the hill.

"Is this the Kingdom of the Dwarfs, Ornella?"

"This is just the beginning of their realm, Izzy. They live underground – we will have to find the secret entrance."

18

Freya

The sun felt pleasantly warm and Izzy lay down on the side of the hill. With the memory of their flight from the Dokkalfar fading, she realised how tired she was now that they were safe. Her eyes were so heavy and she slowly closed them, resting back in the long, dry grass.

Ornella glanced across. "We will eat first, *then* sleep, Izzy."

Izzy nodded awake to see Gillie rummaging around in all the packs with excitement.

"Oh jolly good, what have we got?"

Agnes went over to help him and found some parcels of bread and cheese from the ship, a bit squashed, but still all right, plus a chunk of mushroom.

Izzy took out some seaweed that she had saved from breakfast.

"Ooh, how about sautéed mushrooms and crispy fried seaweed?" said Gillie, rubbing his hands together.

"Go on then, perhaps we could risk a small fire," said Ornella.

Gavin gathered some twigs and lit the fire, while Agnes and Gillie started to prepare the food.

"Have you still got my father's letter safe, Gillie?" asked Ornella.

"Of course, I don't lose *everything*." He patted his chest to make sure it *was* still there. "Thank Freya," he muttered.

"Ornella, who is Freya?" asked Izzy.

"Well, it's a long story, but I suppose it will help to

keep you awake while we wait for our food ...

The Ylfe are the elves of the North … that is who we really are. They lived in Alfheimer, a land of snow-capped mountains, covered with firs, and bluer than blue lakes. They built beautiful castles high up near the snow line, and in the summer wild flowers covered the pastures, while deer, goats, and wolves roamed free. Freya is our god, Izzy. But more than that, she is the land. Alfheimer means 'Elven Home' and it was a gift to our people for Freya's first tooth.

"Why don't you live there now? It sounds amazing."

There was a flash of anger in Ornella's eyes. "The Dokkalfar and dwarfs are to blame for that."

"What did they do?"

"In the beginning the Ljosalfar, Dokkalfar, and the Svartalfar, or dwarfs as you call them, lived together in harmony. But the dark elves grew jealous. They were jealous that we controlled the magic from the teeth and that the dwarfs possessed the Elf shot and runes. So they stole the runes and the recipe for the Elf shot.

We thought that it would restore harmony if we helped the dwarfs to drive them out, but the rift only widened as the dwarfs became suspicious of us too. The Ljosalfar had no choice – we had to take our magic and leave."

"So the dwarfs stayed?"

Ornella gave a snort. "Without magic, there was no invisibility, and the dwarfs soon found what their suspicion had earned them – a lifetime underground, just like our dark brethrin."

Izzy was staring to feel a little concerned at Ornella's growing zeal.

"Isn't that a bit unfair?"

There was a warning flash of Ornella's eyes. "They've only got themselves to blame," she snapped.

"But it's in the past. Couldn't everyone get back together after all this time?"

Gillie came across with a plate of food for both of them. Ornella snatched it out of his hand.

"The food's here now. No more questions, Izzy. Eat. Then we will search for the entrance to the Kingdom of the Dwarfs after we sleep."

Izzy awoke with a start and looked around. The sun was low; it was late in the evening. The others were still sleeping. She wandered off with Orlando, and he started to chase a butterfly. She laughed as he leapt into the air in his efforts to catch it.

"It's not so easy when you're small, is it, Puss? Come on, leave the poor thing alone, I've still got plenty of dried cat food for you."

"Ugh. You spoil all my fun," he grumbled.

Izzy looked up and pointed at the sky. "What's that funny black cloud?"

"I don't know, but it doesn't look right."

"I think it's heading this way," said Izzy. "Let's get Ornella."

They ran back to the campsite and woke Ornella.

They all stood staring into the sky, straining to see in the orange glare from the setting sun.

"That's not a cloud. It looks more like a flock of birds," said Ornella eventually. "Big birds, too, moving fast."

"Seagulls," whispered Izzy. "I just know they're seagulls. Do you think the king of the dark elves has sent them?"

"I think you're right, Izzy. Quickly, back to the others."

They rushed back to the camp, and Ornella scuffed out the fire. Everyone looked up, startled by the sudden urgency.

"Hurry, everyone, gather up your things. We must find a hiding place as soon as possible. Seagulls are on their way. I thought we'd escaped too easily."

"You call that easy?" said Gillie as he rushed around gathering up his gear.

"There's nowhere to hide," said Gavin, looking around desperately. "What will we do?"

"What about the cloaks King Thodrek gave us?" said Agnes. "We could test them out."

"Trust you to be pleased about testing camouflage gear," said Gillie. "But, Agnes, please don't use your home-made cape."

"I'm not. I'm not," she cried.

She looked disappointed as she rummaged in her pack, but she took Gillie's advice for once.

"The cloaks won't be enough," said Ornella. "I'll cast a spell so we look like an outcrop of rocks. There are plenty of those around here."

They all lay quiet, under their cloaks.

"When will we know it's safe?" said Izzy.

"I think we'll know," whispered Ornella. "Seagulls aren't the quietest of birds."

The birds could be heard long before they were near. Their raucous cries filled the air. Closer and closer, the noise grew louder and louder. Soon they were right overhead, squawking, and squabbling. Everyone froze. They tried to keep as still as possible.

Gillie and Izzy huddled together, Orlando between them. Just as the gulls had passed over, Orlando swished his tail under Gillie's nose. Izzy saw the desperate look on his face as he tried not to sneeze. The more he tried to hold it in, the harder it got. And when it came, it was enormous.

"AAACHOO!"

The seagulls wheeled and turned back. They circled the

spot where the group was hiding. Nobody moved.

It was too late. They had been given away. The gulls turned and flew back towards the coast, squawking furiously.

"By the fruits of Quercus!" said Gillie, "I'm so sorry. I couldn't help it."

"Don't worry about it now," said Ornella. "The Dokkalfar have no magic to make themselves invisible. They dare not travel until after dark. We'll be in Cat Belde by then."

Izzy looked up in alarm. "But, Ornella, I saw the king use magic against his brother."

"What? How can that be?"

"It's true. He has a wand and seems very powerful," said Gavin.

For the first time since they had met, Ornella looked uncertain. There was a brief moment of apprehension while everyone waited for Ornella to make a decision.

"We must head for the Bronze Age Circle above Keswick. It is a holy place and will enhance my powers. We'll have to go back to Cat Belde, later."

"How long can you hold them off?" asked Izzy.

"In the stone circle my powers will be greatly magnified. I will be able to protect us, do not fear."

They hurried on under the long shadows of the setting sun, not noticing the scenery now. They had just one thought, to reach the stone circle in time.

Ornella led the way; she didn't seem to tire, but Izzy found it hard to keep up.

"It's not much further," said Ornella. "We should get there just before dark."

They scrambled up the last hill, the stone circle was still in the distance.

Izzy gasped as Ornella unfurled her wings and flew on

ahead. "I've never seen an elf fly before."

"I'd like to fly, too," grumbled Agnes.

"I'm sure we could risk it for that short distance," said Gavin.

"It's all right for you, you're nobility. Ordinary elves don't have unlimited magic."

Gavin smiled and unfurled his wings. "I'll transfer some to you."

He and Agnes lifted Izzy between them high into the air.

Izzy looked back and saw Gillie pick up Orlando, before joining them, flying towards the stones.

19

The Stone Circle

The stones loomed large in the gathering dusk as the group drew near. Izzy felt a strange sense of unease the closer they got.

"They're huge," she gasped. "Will your magic be enough, Ornella?"

"There's a smaller circle within the circle, head for that."

Gavin and Agnes set Izzy down within the ten stones that stood inside the larger circle. Izzy shivered as she looked up. It was like being surrounded by giant craggy skyscrapers, but more than that, she felt them tingling and vibrating. "How long have they been here, Ornella?"

"Since the beginning of time, Izzy."

Gillie dropped Orlando at her feet and Izzy picked him up and hugged him close.

"It's all right, Izzy. We're safe now," said Orlando.

Gavin, Agnes and Gillie took up positions at intervals around the stones, and laid out their weapons in front of them. Ornella went from stone to stone and touched it with Izzy's tooth. As she chanted in her ancient tongue, each stone gave off a faint blue glow and made a quiet hum. When she came to the last stone she looked around.

"Is every one inside? We can't leave once the circle is closed, it will break the spell. Nobody must panic."

"I think we're all prepared," said Gavin, looking at the others.

Izzy, Agnes and Gillie nodded. Ornella closed the last stone, and they waited.

Gavin went over to Izzy. "Here, Izzy, wear my aventail for protection."

Izzy wobbled under the weight of the helmet, but was glad of it nonetheless.

It wasn't long before they heard the sound of marching feet and clanking armour. Then, in the distance they could see a small party heading towards them.

"Ornella, be careful, it's the King of the Dokkalfar himself," Izzy called out.

As he approached, Izzy trembled. His face looked as dark as his black soul. He stood looking at the circle of glowing stones.

"So, I see you are trying to use magic to evade capture," he sneered. "You must surely know that you cannot escape from me. You wouldn't have got away in the first place if my traitor brother hadn't helped you."

He began to chant. A wispy thread of green light emanated from the tip of his wand. It wound about the stone circle.

"What's he doing?" whispered Izzy.

"I don't know yet," said Ornella. "Hold fast everyone."

The green light gradually took on the form of ghostly shapes. Hideous, half-eaten away faces leered at them menacingly from the darkness. The billowing shreds of their winding sheets only partially covered their skeletal forms. Izzy cowered in abject terror.

Agnes let out a piercing scream. "It's the spirits of the dead. We'll all be killed. Run."

"My sword's passing right through them," shouted Gillie, swinging his blade back and forth. "We have to get out of here."

Gavin and Gillie thrashed with their swords, hacking and stabbing. They twisted and turned. Panic spread through the little group as the ghostly figures glided about, swirling around and around, instilling dreadful fear and loathing.

Agnes broke. She started to run for an opening between the stones. Gavin and Gillie were about to follow.

"NO! NO!" screamed Ornella. "It's a trick. Don't leave the circle. I can only keep us safe if we stay in the circle."

"Help. Leave me alone," yelled Agnes, spinning wildly with her stick.

She almost hit Gillie in her panic.

Izzy suddenly felt dizzy, staggered and fell to the ground.

"Izzy! What's happened to Izzy?" cried Ornella.

Izzy lay on the ground, motionless. Orlando stood over her, one great paw on her arm. Then she started to mutter, half to herself. "Nan? Nanny Ellen, help us please."

The figure of an elderly woman started to appear, and a warm rose-coloured glow radiated from her. It spread outwards towards the stones, and as it spread, the hideous, ghostly figures started to fade.

The King of the Dokkalfar was consumed with rage. "How have you managed to defeat my magic?"

Izzy sat up and looked around, just as the king ordered his guards to attack.

"Caspare, fire at will," he growled to his captain.

The men under Caspare levelled their bows. At his command they fired between the stones. The arrows flew through the air, but as they reached the humming eerie blue aura, they fell harmlessly to the ground. The king looked as though he was going to explode.

"I see there is someone new in your group. Someone royal perhaps, who knows the ancient lore. Who has the temerity to challenge me?"

Ornella walked to the edge of the circle. She looked every inch a princess as she faced the dark king.

"I am Princess Ornella, daughter of King Thodrek. Beware whom you choose to attack. If any harm should come to this group, you will have a civil war on your conscience and my father will not rest until your head has parted company from your shoulders. You have already alienated a brother – do not alienate the whole of elf kind as your ancestors did once before."

"How dare you speak to me in such a manner. You realise you have sealed your fate, along with those scum who serve you."

The king turned to his men and barked an order. "Caspare, don't fire until I have weakened their defences. Be ready to move as soon as there is a breach in the circle. I want them alive. I want them back on Anglesey, and I want them back in my dungeons. And you, my precious princess, will pay for your impudence."

Gillie got up and stood beside Ornella.

"We would rather die, before we'd allow you to capture our princess."

There was a 'hear, hear' from Gavin, a murmur of assent from Agnes, and Izzy and Orlando nodded.

The King of the Dokkalfar stood a few paces away from the stone circle. He bowed his head as though deep in thought, then slowly raised his arms and head while quietly chanting the ancient elvish language. The runes on his crown glowed and a great stream of golden light issued from his black ebony wand. It poured onto the nearest opening between the stones. Sparks flew upwards into the night sky. A terrifying display of coloured lights bounced off the blue aura surrounding the group. The noise was deafening.

"How much longer can your magic stand up to the king's assault?" said Izzy.

"I don't know. I thought I could hold us, but he's very

strong. What bothers me is he shouldn't have any magic at all."

At that moment the blue glow between the stones began to flicker, like a flame that was guttering, about to go out.

"Make ready to fight," cried Ornella.

Caspare and his men also made ready to fire. But as the breach widened, Gavin and Agnes were ahead of them.

Two of the king's men fell; wounded by the arrows they fired simultaneously.

"Good shot," cried Gavin.

"All my practice has paid off," said Agnes. "Just like Robin Hood."

"Robin who?"

"Never mind, I'll tell you later."

The attackers were not to be taken by surprise again. They dropped to the ground for cover. This time Gillie fired, and missed.

Ornella hurled a streak of blue light through the breach. The king quickly deflected it with a stream of gold. The two beams arced, intertwined and a myriad of sparks shot off in all directions.

Gavin, Gillie and Agnes continued to fire. But the light from the beams was blinding. They could hardly see where to aim.

Suddenly the guards rushed the breach. A couple caught arrows and went down, but several broke through – they were in the circle. One rushed Izzy and picked her up.

Orlando launched himself at the guard's leg, claws out, spitting and biting. He clung on with determined ferocity. The elf dropped Izzy immediately, his screams blocking out the noise from the exploding beams of magic.

Gavin, Agnes and Gillie were fighting hand to hand, but the odds were not with them.

Ornella was tiring, the constant effort draining her. She slumped to her knees. "How are you doing this? Why is your power so strong?" she asked, and her arm fell for an instant, dropping her guard.

The king strode forward, and seizing his chance to disarm her, he knocked the wand from her hand and stood on it. Grabbing her plait, he pulled her head back.

"Your power has made you arrogant, Princess. You will

regret the way you spoke to me. Time to die." He pulled out a dagger and held it to her throat.

There was nothing the others could do. They were outnumbered, fighting for their lives.

Izzy had her back pressed against a stone; Orlando crouched in front ready to attack. Two guards closed in. She had no escape.

Suddenly thwack, thwack – the sound of darts thudding into flesh. Then more darts whickered through the air. The king went down, dropping Ornella. He bent over in pain. The guards near Izzy fell, clutching their stomachs in agony.

Izzy realised they were no longer alone. Large, stocky, shapes loomed out of the darkness. They were larger than elves, but smaller than humans.

Flights of arrows were fired in both directions. Before long the battle was over. The Dokkalfar arrows had hit home many times, but the Elf shot did nothing to affect the newcomers.

The whole group stood quietly, waiting for the leader to approach. When he did, to everyone's surprise, he went down onto one knee to Ornella.

"King Gregorian of the Svartalfar has sent me to your aid. My name is Cronar, I am cousin to the king. You will come with us now, the king wishes to speak with you."

Ornella recovered quickly, and stood up. "Our thanks to you, Cronar. I too, wish to speak with your king. My father, King Thodrek, has sent us here on an important mission that affects all of elfkind."

"Then please follow me, Your Highness, before the whole of Keswick is awake and racing up here to see what all the noise is about. Although I see you have brought your own human child with you. We have heard rumours about this child. Is she indeed the child of the prophecy?"

"Forgive me, Cronar – now is neither the time nor the place." Ornella nodded towards the dark king and placed her finger against her lips.

The dwarfs tied the guards and their king together. It was hardly necessary; they were still bent over in agony. Cronar ordered his dwarfs to carry the injured, while he took the ebony wand and weapons from the king. The king's silver circlet caught his eye, and he removed that too, under a tirade of abuse from the king. Then he led the way back into the darkness of the fells, with everyone following as quickly as they could.

Izzy was exhausted after the battle, and stumbled along after the others as best she could. A journey that had started with a simple idea to visit the dwarfs had turned into the worst kind of nightmare. When would it end?

20

The Derwentwater Dwarfs

Izzy ran beside the dwarfs, legs pumping mechanically, her curiosity the only thing keeping her going. The dwarfs were so different to her friends, she could hardly believe they were related. The light and dark elves were slim and beautiful, but these elves were large and stocky, you could even say fat, as long as they didn't hear you.

With their long beards, leather jerkins, and belts full of weaponry, the dwarfs looked almost identical to pictures in storybooks. Izzy wondered how that could be if no one could see them. Although there was one difference, all these dwarfs wore leggings. It wasn't the best look, but it probably wasn't wise to give people with so many axes and daggers fashion advice.

Izzy sidled closer. "Excuse me, sir, but how did you know to rescue us?"

"There's nothing above or below ground that we are not aware of in our own realm, little Miss. But you were making so much noise it would have been strange had we not been alerted. We've been tracking your group since you entered our territory."

Cronar's gruff manner relaxed as Izzy trotted alongside him, chatting happily.

"May I see the king's circlet?" interrupted Ornella, taking advantage of his good mood.

Cronar held out the crown almost automatically, first showing it to Izzy and then handing it to Ornella. "There are white gems embedded in it, I took it just for safety, of course."

Ornella examined the crown closely. "These aren't gems, they're shards of teeth. How did the dark elves get hold of them?"

"Probably stole 'em, the same way those scoundrels got our runes and Elf shot," said Cronar."

"Yes," said Izzy. "Why weren't you affected by the Elf shot? You were all hit several times."

"Enough, enough," said Cronar, laughing, "our king will answer all your questions. We still have a way to go yet, and we must make good time."

Izzy dropped back and fell in beside Agnes and Gillie. "Are you all right, Gillie?"

Gillie nodded, puffing a little at the pace.

"How about you, Agnes?"

"Do you think they make all their own weapons?" whispered Agnes, her eyes glittering at the dwarfs' array of equipment.

Izzy laughed. "I'll take that as a 'yes' too."

It wasn't long before they reached the side of the fell. In front of them Derwentwater shone in the moonlight.

"Almost home," said Cronar. "The entrance is on the other side of the lake, at the foot of the fell."

The dwarfs pulled well-hidden rafts from the bushes that surrounded the shore. They sat on both sides, each with a long wooden oar. When Izzy and the group were on board, the dwarfs pushed off. Rowing in perfect unison, almost as if they were automatons, the dwarfs powered the rafts quickly and quietly across the lake.

Cronar turned to Izzy. "Do you know of a human called Beatrix Potter?"

"Yes, I've got several of her books."

"She bequeathed all this area to the National Trust, for us." Cronar pointed to the woods on the left. "A great agreement, it means we can live here in peace."

"You were friends with Beatrix Potter?"

"Not just friends, *business* partners," said Cronar with pride. "We gave her all our best stories in exchange. Some rare humans still have imagination enough to believe in us when they become adults."

Before long they reached the lower slopes of Cat Belde. Cronar went to a grassy bank between two outcrops of rocks and started chanting. Runes appeared in the grass, glowing faintly orange. Then an opening appeared in the bank that showed a large room … not a tunnel or steps, as Izzy had expected.

Cronar led them in. "Everyone ready?" he said. "Hold on to your stomachs."

Izzy was grateful for the warning as they plummeted downwards. After the experience in the realm of the Dokkalfar, she was expecting dark, damp, narrow tunnels, but as she stepped out of the lift she was amazed at the enormity of the hall. Huge, arched ceilings had been carved and ornately decorated from solid rock, and it was surprisingly warm and well lit.

The prisoners were taken away to holding cells on a different level, while Izzy and the group were led to comfortable, well furnished apartments with every possible convenience. Orlando immediately rushed in, jumped up on a sumptuous leather recliner and padded the cushions.

Cronar bowed to Ornella. "I hope this will be suitable for you, Princess?"

Ornella laughed. "I think our furry friend has already given his seal of approval."

"Very well," said Cronar. "You will meet with King Gregorian in the morning. There is hot water and refreshments if you need them, for now I bid you all goodnight."

Izzy was nearly asleep on her feet by this time and stumbled over to one of the beds. They'd finally made it, and if Cronar was anything to go by, King Gregorian would surely be able to answer all their questions about the crisis of magic.

In the morning they were all taken to a large dining room that had a buffet spread out on an enormous table. They helped themselves to a lavish cooked breakfast, followed by pancakes with syrup and fresh fruit.

"I must say we've been treated very well," said Agnes. "I thought it would be miserable underground."

"It's nothing like I expected either," said Gillie, finishing his second nectar and ginger draught. "By the way, Izzy, what happened to you at the stone circle?"

"What do you mean?"

"Don't you know? You started talking – asking for help. Then an elderly woman appeared, and a pink glow seemed to chase away the evil spirits."

"I remember something about my nan, but I thought it was just a dream."

"I told you you'd begin to discover your powers in time," said Ornella.

Izzy sat pensively while the others continued to eat.

"These pancakes and syrup are delicious," said Agnes. "I'll be too heavy to fly if I eat any more."

There was a knock on the door, and Cronar entered.

"Princess Ornella, and honoured guests, I do hope you have all slept well, and enjoyed our humble provisions. If you are ready, I will escort you to the king."

They followed Cronar along bright, well-ventilated corridors, until they reached two large oak doors that were carved exquisitely with all manner of animals and trees. Two dwarfs were on guard and stood to attention when

Cronar marched up to them.

"I have Princess Ornella and her party to see the king, would you please see if he is ready to receive them?"

The group waited outside for a moment until they were told to enter. The guards opened the doors, and Izzy gazed in awe at the comfort and grandeur of the king's chamber. Books lined one wall from top to bottom, and the stone floor was covered in brightly-coloured, luxurious rugs. At the far end of the chamber the king was sitting very comfortably, his large belly resting on the table in front of him, while he browsed through what looked like maps.

"Ah there you are, Princess Ornella, I'm very pleased to meet you at last. Of course I know your father from long, long ago, but we haven't had an occasion to get together for years."

The king looked very much like Cronar, except his hair and beard were red and he was much, much bigger. He had a friendly and kind face, didn't wear a crown, nor did he look kingly in any respect. Except for superficial appearances, nothing about the dwarfs seemed as Izzy expected.

"Your Majesty," said Ornella, and curtsied, "we are pleased to meet you. Let me introduce Gillie and Agnes, they are wood elves from the Great Forest, Gavin Goshawk, who volunteered to help us, and, last but not least, Izzy Green, a human child, and her cat, Orlando."

Izzy curtsied, and the others bowed, including Agnes.

"Don't bother with all that nonsense," the king bellowed, "come and sit down over here."

He gestured to the large sofas and chairs. The king seemed to be very jolly and very welcoming; just like Cronar.

But at the back of her mind Izzy started to feel that something was not quite genuine about his friendliness.

21

A Falling Out

Izzy's sense of mistrust continued to grow as the king patted her on the head, flattered Ornella, and shook Gillie and Gavin warmly by the hand. What it was, she couldn't quite tell, but instinctively she knew she could not trust the friendly, jolly king, whereas she knew without doubt that she would trust Elander with her life.

"I'll send for refreshments," said the king. "I know you've only just had breakfast, but I'm sure you could find room for a few fairy cakes and mead. I certainly can." He rubbed his ample stomach in demonstration, while Cronar rushed off to organise the food.

"Now, Princess Ornella, what made you travel the whole length of England to see me? It must be important, and with a human child in tow, that will need some explaining."

"We have come to see you about …"

"AND BRING SOME PIXIE CAKES," the king bellowed to Cronar. He turned back to Ornella. "I'm so sorry, do go on."

"… flying spheres," stammered Ornella. "They are stealing the teeth from the human children. Gillie has a letter from my father that explains everything."

Gillie stepped forward and took the letter from his tunic.

King Gregorian read it and shook his head. "This is all very strange. Our understanding is that our silver spheres are supposed to make things better, not worse."

"So you *are* making the spheres?" gasped Izzy.

She was suddenly aware that the king was staring at her intensely. It dispelled any impression of his outward joviality.

"Your Majesty," Ornella stepped in quickly and continued. "What are you doing with the teeth?"

"No, no, you don't understand," said the king, turning back to Ornella. "We only make the spheres. We send them off to a distribution depot just outside of London. A large country house, Redcliffe Manor, I believe. The company uses the spheres to collect the teeth, not us."

"Sire, what company would that be?" asked Gillie.

"The Company of Goblins."

"I knew it, I knew it," said Ornella, with barely concealed satisfaction. "I just knew goblins were behind everything. Your Majesty, this is the proof I need to convince my father that we must go to war, immediately."

Izzy thought it best just to listen as the king continued.

"Don't be so hasty, child," said King Gregorian, looking alarmed. "This will make things better for everyone. It has for us. The Chief Executive of the company, Khaverin Fielderial, came to me some time ago with a proposal that we manufacture the spheres. A most charming goblin and a welcome change from the days when goblins constantly waged war. He said they've taken inspiration from humans and set up a wonderful new company, St Onomans. He said that collecting the teeth with our spheres would greatly increase efficiency, then he would distribute the magic fairly and equally to all."

Agnes, who hadn't been paying much attention until now, suddenly stood up. "That's a brilliant idea. Why should the nobility get most of the magic and lowly wood elves just get what's left over?"

"Agnes, you don't know the full story," urged Gillie, glaring at her. "We should wait until we know more about this. You heard the flower fairies, they weren't very happy with the situation, nor were the house elves, or Landwihta."

"That might just mean the magic hasn't been distributed yet," argued Agnes. "When it is, everything will be all right."

"And what about the Dokkalfar?" reasoned Gillie. "It's obvious the goblins gave Ragnestar some children's teeth, and look what happened, he almost *killed* us. Perhaps there is good reason why only the nobility have the responsibility for magic."

"Well, we all know why you're on the same side as royalty." Agnes looked at Gillie and then Ornella. "You're biased because you have a 'special interest'."

Gillie went red, "I think you've said enough, Agnes, I just don't think we should be hasty, nothing more."

There was an awkward pause, and Izzy went over to the king. "Please, Your Majesty, my father works for St Onomans. Are you saying that goblins run his company?"

At that moment great platters of food and drink arrived, much to the king's obvious relief. He was starting to look uncomfortable with all the questions. "Help yourselves everyone, plenty here to fill a corner or two. Now, my dear, as I understand it, the goblins were so taken by St Onomans they set up their own company and called it by the same name. As you're human, you probably don't understand that for a goblin, or any magical creature for that matter, to run a human company would be impossible. I mean, they would have to somehow never be seen."

Izzy frowned. "But with modern technology ..."

The king laughed. "No, no, no, quite impossible. Anyway, the Goblin King, or more correctly, Chief Executive Khaverin Fielderial, did tell me that he was going to get in touch with King Thodrek about the distribution of the magic. But I suppose he hasn't got around to it yet, he's very busy you know. I'm sure it will all work out for the best, just wait and see."

"Thank you, Your Majesty," Izzy bobbed a curtsy and returned to her seat.

"Your Majesty, what will you do with the Dokkalfar?" asked Gavin.

"Set them free of course, it would be illegal to do anything else. However, that battle you had last night broke Clause 4, Unauthorised Light Pollution, so it requires us to confiscate that pretty circlet of silver and the beautiful wand he had. We have to stick to the letter of the law, after all we don't go around taking nice things just because we want them.

Now, before you entered, I was looking at the maps of our underground system. I think the closest I can get you to your Island is going to be my nephew's area in Cornwall – we still do a fair bit of mining there, you know. I'll give you a letter for him. I'm sure he'll arrange for one of our sailing vessels to take you the rest of the way."

He started scribbling on a sheet of paper, signed it with a flourish, stuffed it into an envelope and handed it to Ornella.

"Thank you very much, Your Majesty," said Ornella. "But would you please consider not making any more spheres until after I've had a chance to talk to my father?"

"No, no, no, my dear. We would be breaking our contract with the goblins for no good reason … the law's the law. You really should try one of these pixie cakes you know. They're very good."

Taking another bite, he continued. "Your concern is sincere, but I fear, misplaced. Our business relationship with the goblins has brought wealth and prosperity to all in my kingdom. Let's just wait and see whether your father has heard from the Chief Executive by the time you get back. Now goodbye, it's been very interesting talking to all of you, and the special child. Cronar will take you to the underground railway."

Cronar led the way out of the chamber. The meeting with the king was over, and they had been dismissed.

"Our underground railway is very fast. You'll be in Cornwall in no time at all," said Cronar. He led them along the corridors until they arrived at another lift, and then pressed the button for it to come.

"Another steep drop I'm afraid," he said as they all piled in. "The railway runs from the lower level."

Agnes had been avoiding looking at Gillie or Ornella since they'd left the king's chamber. She stood in the corner of the lift stubbornly looking straight ahead.

"What's wrong, Agnes?" whispered Izzy.

Agnes remained silent. The doors opened and everyone made their way into the tunnel. Izzy stayed with Agnes and they followed a short distance behind the others.

"You don't understand," said Agnes. "It's them and us, the wealthy versus the poor. The users of powerful magic and ordinary elves who have to ration what they use."

"What was that?" said Gillie, looking around.

"You heard," snapped Agnes.

"Agnes, what would you do with powerful magic?" said Gillie. "You've always had enough to heal the plants and trees. What do you want to do? Fight evil kings, and fly on falcons?"

"I might do."

Gillie gasped in exasperation. "Well, I think you owe Ornella an apology; she has always treated us as equals. And there's good reason to be cautious about this Company of Goblins."

"Ornella *has* been very kind," said Izzy.

"All right, I am sorry about that. I just never took you all for Goblinists, especially you, Gillie."

Gillie was brought to a standstill. He stood in silence, his mouth wide open.

Izzy tried to hold on to Agnes, but she defiantly stormed off and pushed her way to the front of the group.

Orlando jumped out of her way and trotted back to Izzy. "What's up with Agnes? She was in such a hurry she almost stepped on my tail."

"I'll tell you later, Puss. There's no time now – we'll miss the train."

Gillie remained motionless, looking bewildered. "I, I, I've never seen her like this before," he finally stammered.

"Come on, Gillie, we have to go," said Izzy pulling his arm. "We can sort it out once we're on the train."

Orlando got behind Gillie and butted his head against his legs. Gillie shuffled forward a couple of steps and then stopped.

"This calls for drastic measures," said Orlando.

"YEEEOWWWW," cried Gillie, finally stumbling into motion.

"Ah, they have so many uses," chuckled Orlando, retracting his claws.

They hurried along the corridor and caught up to the others just in time to board a carriage for the journey back home.

22

The Journey Home

Izzy slept for the first part of the journey back to the south. When she woke she clambered out of her sleeping birth. Orlando was still curled up, dozing away, as always. Her friends were all still asleep too, or perhaps refusing to come out due to the earlier arguments.

Izzy decided to stretch her legs a little and wandered through the carriages while the train sped along. As with everything about the dwarfs, it was lavishly decorated. Deep mahogany wood panels, inlaid with geometric designs of lighter wood, made up much of the interior.

After making her way through the sleeping births and dining area, Izzy finally found the dwarfs. They were in a sitting room, a compartment that occupied an entire carriage. They welcomed her in and were keen to show her around. Bookcases lined the walls, but in the centre of the carriage on a golden pedestal, stood something far more interesting. The dwarfs called it a mechanatome. Similar in shape to a large crystal ball, but with glowing, spinning cogs, the dwarfs were eager to show it off. Through its intricate mechanics it was able to store all manner of music, stories, and could even project images on to a screen.

The dwarfs were very clever, but one thing was clear, all this stuff required a lot of money. It was understandable why the goblins' proposal had been so welcomed by King Gregorian.

Izzy joined the dwarfs at their large circular table, and listened to their stories of ancient lore and dwarfish heroism. Another thing became very clear, the dwarfs loved to talk about themselves. It was just as well, because there was no point in looking out of the windows, the only view was mile upon mile of rock. It was only when every now and then they passed a station, that she could get a true impression of their speed. She tried to read the station names as they rushed by the window, but it was impossible, they were gone in the blink of an eye. It was no wonder the train was called 'The Golden Bullet'.

When they arrived in Cornwall, some hours later, Izzy disembarked the train and joined her friends on the platform. The king's nephew strode up to meet them. He was a jolly dwarf, his hair and beard as red as his uncle's. In fact he looked almost the same as his uncle, but he didn't have such a large girth … not many dwarfs did.

"Call me Gringold, pleased to meet you all," he said bowing low. "My uncle sent me notification of your arrival on our telegraph. But I still need to see his letter; it's Clause 12 of our transport code."

"You're very security conscious," said Gillie. "But how do you know the letter's from the king? We could have forged it."

"That's easy," said Gringold shaking out the envelope. "Cake crumbs."

They all laughed, for the first time since their disagreement. But the moment was brief, and the tension in the group quickly returned.

"This way then, our sailing ship is waiting for you. You'll arrive at your palace first thing in the morning."

Before long they were underway. The dwarfs' ship didn't look like any vessel Izzy had seen before. In place of a sail there were two rotating cylinders, the dwarfs called them turbo sails. Even when making use of something as natural as the wind, their methods were very mechanical.

Izzy wanted to talk about the Goblin Company, and the division that had occurred between her friends over the equal distribution of magic, but everyone was steering clear of the topic. Gavin looked especially down, while Gillie was avoiding being alone with Ornella, or even speaking much to her. Izzy was upset, the spirit of their friendship felt tarnished. It was as though none of the adventures they'd been through, which had brought them closer together, had ever happened.

The next morning rose bright and clear. Izzy went on deck to catch the first glimpse of the palace and found Ornella already up. The princess was clearly as anxious as she was to get back.

Izzy stood beside Ornella, and together they watched the Island of the Ljosalfar as it sped by on their right.

"You know, Ornella, I don't care what that dwarf king says, I suspect the two companies are the same. He said the goblin in charge was Khaverin Fielderial, and my dad's director's initials are KFC. It's too much of a co-incidence. And my father's changed since he went to work there. I *hate* St Onomans."

"I'm with you, Izzy. I don't understand how they're doing it, but if there *was* a way I'm sure the goblins would find it. *I* hate goblins."

Izzy paused, taken aback by Ornella's zeal. "You don't suppose Agnes is right, and we're being Goblinists, do you?"

"My mother was killed by goblins," snapped Ornella. "Agnes only has the freedoms she enjoys, because we defeated those vile creatures in the wars. Trust me, Izzy, they're up to no good."

"But isn't it wrong to judge them by what they did in

the past?"

"A goblin never changes its colour, Izzy. They're green and always will be."

Izzy was about to reply, when she was suddenly aware of a babble of voices drifting across the water. The noise grew steadily, as the vessel drew closer to the shore. Izzy and Ornella exchanged worried looks.

When they rounded the corner and came into the bay, Izzy saw the beach was crammed with figures. Magical creatures of all types were camped out on the sand and between the rocks. It seemed as though every single one of the king's subjects was there.

A merlin came flying across to the ship. Izzy saw him first as he swooped down on to the rail. It was Ornella's hunting bird, Regan.

"My princess," he cried. He tipped his head to one side, and the flash of brown over his eyes made him look very fierce. "You've come back just in time. Things are nearly at breaking point. Every day more and more creatures arrive in the hope that the king will solve their problems, and they all need feeding."

"Calm down, Regan, I'm sure things will be put right soon," said Ornella, but she didn't look at all confident.

She climbed onto his back and held out her hand. "Come on, Izzy. Let's see what we can do to help."

Gillie came up on deck just as they took off.

"I'll catch up with you and the others later," called Izzy.

As they flew over the beach there was pandemonium below them. It was hard to see the shoreline through the mass of creatures. Different groups were arguing with each other, vying for the best positions nearest the palace. The noise was almost deafening. Cofgodas had banded together into groups. Fruit and flower fairies were pushed aside in the crush and looked completely bewildered. Other creatures frantically changed shape, from trees into deer, then foxes, and back into trees again.

Ornella glanced back over her shoulder. "It's the Landwihta, shape shifters; they've gone a little mad. They're solitary creatures, and don't like being this close to others."

Izzy pointed to a group that looked like beautiful children from the front, but had the hollowed out backs of trees from behind. "Who are they, Ornella?"

"Oh no, it's the Huldrufolk, Izzy. If they're here, who is left to guard the spirits of the trees? The situation is worse than I feared."

Regan landed on Ornella's balcony. She and Izzy hopped off and raced to King Thodrek's chambers. Ornella almost skidded past the door in her hurry, but just managed to stop in time. She banged on it impatiently.

"Father, can I come in? Izzy's here, too."

The king opened the door, gave his daughter a hug and welcomed Izzy.

"Oh, my dears, I'm so glad to see you both. Things have gone from bad to worse since you left. Every day more and more magical creatures arrive."

He looked distraught and weary, as though he hadn't slept for many nights. "I really don't know what we'll do. What did you find out? I hope you have good news."

"Alas, no, Father. There is much to tell you." Ornella outlined everything that had happened since they had left. "And the goblins have some harebrained scheme about sharing our magic," she continued. "They're the ones behind St Onomans, too."

"What? Izzy's father's company?" said the king.

"Well, not exactly," said Izzy. "King Gregorian claimed they just copied it."

"That's very strange," said the king, "two companies with the same name. But how is this scheme going to work?"

"I don't know, Father. They're calling it 'equality of magic for all'. I only know that King Gregorian said the Chief Executive of St Onomans would be in touch with you."

"How dare he; equality for all," the king spluttered. He looked as though he was going to explode. "Chief Executive – is that what he's calling himself now? How dare he steal our magic, and then presume to offer it back."

The reaction of the king to the idea of freely available magic was a little unnerving. Izzy was confused. *Was* she on the right side in all this after all?

Ornella paced up and down. "I don't think we have any choice but to go to war, Father. We must act while we still have the chance."

Izzy's misgivings couldn't be contained any longer. "Your Majesty, shouldn't you at least find out what the Goblin Chief Executive is offering, first?"

Ornella's disdain was clearly visible.

"I mean, not that you should accept what he says," said Izzy, trying to diffuse the tension. "Just that it's important to have all the information before you make a decision."

"What more information do we need?" cried Ornella. "We must act. We must take back the magic, *now*."

"Enough!" The king held up his hand. "Izzy is right. We cannot act in haste. We cannot start a conflict without all the facts."

Izzy breathed a sigh of relief. All the same, she was becoming more and more uncertain whether the monarchy was any better than the goblins.

23

Uproar at the Palace

Izzy was worried that Ornella would take matters into her own hands; what if she lost her as a friend? There was already a rift developing with Agnes. As she tried to think of something to say, there was a knock at the door. The king called out to enter, and Elander appeared.

Ornella's hand moved towards her sword.

"Wait!" cried Izzy, running to Elander's side.

"Father?" Ornella hesitated.

"As impetuous as ever, just like your mother," said the king shaking his head. "At ease, daughter. Elander and his men brought my ship back and have pledged me their allegiance. I don't know what we would have done without their help. We would have been overrun by now, if not for them."

Elander bowed to Ornella, "I am at your service, Your Highness." He turned to Izzy and smiled. "Hello, little one. You're still jumping in the way of swords to protect others, I see."

Izzy felt a little embarrassed and nodded, smiling gingerly.

"Now, what news, Elander?" said the king.

"A seagull arrived a few minutes ago with a letter from St Onomans, Your Majesty."

Elander took the letter from under his silver and grey armour and handed it to the king, bowing as he did so.

"This letter requests a meeting next Wednesday. The Chief Executive will be coming in person. We are to send our reply back by seagull." The king handed the letter to

Ornella.

The noise outside suddenly grew louder, there were gasps, and then cheering. Izzy, the king, Elander and Ornella hurried over to the balcony. To their amazement seagulls were dropping dozens and dozens of leaflets.

Everyone on the beach was running and scrabbling for them. The creatures that had managed to grab a leaflet were cheering and laughing, while others were still rushing to get one.

"We need to know what they say," said Izzy.

"Indeed we do. Go with her, Ornella, get me one of those leaflets as soon as you can," ordered the king.

Izzy and Ornella sped out of the chamber. As they hurtled down the spiral steps they met Gillie, Agnes, Gavin and Orlando, who were climbing up from below.

Agnes had a handful of leaflets in her grasp. She waved them around with great satisfaction, then thrust them at Izzy and Ornella, her face jubilant.

"Look," she cried. "Free magic for all. Everything will be all right now, no more rationing, we'll all be able to fly again, whenever we want."

"Let me see that," growled Ornella, snatching a leaflet out of Agnes' hand.

Ornella turned and raced back up to her father's chamber.

Gillie bent down and picked up one of the leaflets.

"Have you read all of this, Agnes?" he pointed to some small print at the bottom.

Conditions apply; magic credit can be extended to all.

"I've watched a lot of programmes on television, that's just normal business practice." Agnes snorted dismissively, and marched off after Ornella.

Izzy went over to stroke Orlando, but he turned his

back on her.

"What's wrong, Orlando?"

"You left me behind on the ship." Orlando looked most put out.

"I'm sorry, Puss, it happened so quickly. I didn't have a chance to come and get you. Besides, you went off with Ornella as well."

"I'm a cat, it's allowed."

"Come on, don't sulk. We have to catch up with the others." She smoothed his silky coat and he quickly forgave her. Izzy picked him up and rushed back up the steps.

Before long they were all together in the king's chamber.

"I've just sent the reply," said the king. "The sooner we meet with this executive the better. What do the leaflets say?"

"Free magic for all," groaned Ornella, handing the note to her father. "Look."

"Just as I feared, it will be impossible to stop this now everyone knows what's on offer."

"Can't we get to the teeth before the spheres?" said Gillie.

"I don't think so," said the king, "those mechanical spheres are very efficient. Our method is rather out of date, I suppose. Anyway, I'm glad to see all of you safely back."

"But couldn't you offer equality of magic, too?" said Izzy "You *are* the king."

"*Share* magic?" scoffed the king. "We're royalty, we can't share with ordinary elves; we need magic to rule."

Izzy felt a jolt in her stomach at the king's response. Doubt and uncertainty filled her mind and she swallowed hard. "But if that's what the majority want, isn't it the right thing to do, Your Majesty?"

"Royalty do what's right? Humph, fine chance," grumbled Agnes.

"That is quite enough, young elf. If you're not careful you'll find there is a limit to my tolerance," said the king, raising his voice.

"But what about everyone outside?" said Izzy. "Agnes isn't the only ... "

"I have a lot to think about," interrupted the king. "Elander, will you ask Lord Falcon to come to my chamber? I need his counsel. Now, if that is everything, I'll bid you all good day."

It was clear that the topic of magic equality had been closed.

Izzy followed everyone back into the corridor. Apart from Agnes, the mood of the group was sombre.

"If you don't mind, I think I'll go down to the beach to wait," said Agnes. "I'm not royalty – I'm just a simple wood elf. I should be with my own kind."

"As you wish," said Ornella.

"But, Agnes, you don't have to go," said Izzy. "I'm sure we can work this out, at least come and have some lunch with us, first."

"No. I think it's for the best." Agnes shot a look at Ornella. "I won't be hypocritical and accept hospitality from people who don't believe in sharing magic."

"Agnes, please don't go," pleaded Izzy. "You're upsetting everyone."

"You don't understand, you're just a child," said Agnes abruptly. "How about you, Gillie, are you coming?"

Gillie seemed dreadfully torn and looked back and forth between Agnes and Ornella. "I'm sorry, Agnes, Ornella's our friend. And I can't believe you just said that to Izzy."

Agnes turned her back and walked away, her head

down. Izzy was very hurt, but wondered if Agnes was the one crying.

"Well, that was for the best," said Ornella, hotly.

Gavin suddenly mumbled something about having to go and visit his goshawk, and rushed off.

"Ornella, look what you've done," said Izzy.

"Me? How is that my fault? So you're siding with Agnes and the goblins now, are you?"

"No, Ornella, but all Agnes wanted was a little bit of equality, perhaps she had a point?"

"It's not that simple, Izzy. Perhaps Agnes was right and you *are* just a child. Gillie understands, don't you, Gillie?"

They both looked around. Gillie was just visible for a moment, before disappearing around a corner.

They stood in silence for a moment, and Orlando smarmed himself around their legs. "Please, don't argue, not you two as well."

Izzy looked down at her hands – they were starting to shake a little. She took a deep breath to try to calm herself. "Everyone keeps saying I don't understand, but I think I finally do. Lord Falcon once said my power existed only because of choice. Can't you see Ornella, so does yours? You only rule because the people choose to follow you, you can't force them to give their loyalty. Remember the Dokkalfar – do you want a revolution here, too?"

"How can you even say that, Izzy? I'm nothing like Ragnestar. I'm simply trying to protect my people, you obviously can't see ..."

"Please STOP," Orlando called out. "My ears are starting to hurt. I can't take it anymore."

Izzy bent down and picked him up, a single tear rolled down her cheek as she buried her face in his deep, silky fur. "I'm sorry, Puss. It's just that for the first time since we left home I don't know what to do. What should I do?"

Orlando purred and gave her face a lick. "I'm not sure I can help. I'm just a cat. Besides it would only be one more opinion, and it seems to me that no one really knows for sure what the goblins are up to."

"That's it, Orlando. You're a genius."

"I am? Well, I mean, yes of course I am. What did I say?"

"No one really knows what the goblins are up to," said Izzy.

"I do," said Ornella.

"No you don't, Ornella. Orlando is right, no one knows for sure. But we need to find out. What we need is proof."

"That's all very well, Izzy, but how? How are we going to get proof?" said Ornella.

"St Onomans. Everything started with them. The penthouse, the voice, the initials of the chief executive; I know what I have to do now. I have to go back there and get some evidence to convince everyone."

"I don't know about that, Izzy," said Ornella. I can't allow you to put yourself in that kind of danger. What if you got caught?"

"Ornella, please, after all the dangers we've been through already, I'm sure I could manage it. If you don't help me I'll just do it anyway, you know I will. It's my birthday tomorrow. I could ask my dad to take me to the office as a birthday treat. I can get you the proof before the king meets with the goblins, it's the perfect opportunity."

"I'll go with you, in your backpack," said Orlando.

"I suppose I could give you an invisibility potion, and if you did get the chance, you could slip away," said Ornella. "Very well, let's go and arrange for Lord Falcon to take you back. Just don't tell anyone about the plan, not even my father."

"Why not?"

"He would never allow it, and we still suspect there is a spy in the palace, the fewer people that know the better.

Izzy nodded.

"Good, and when you have the proof, you'll see I was right."

"Please, promise to wait until I have some evidence before doing anything," said Izzy.

"I don't know why you'd think I'd do anything rash."

Izzy and Orlando gave each other a look as Ornella turned and marched off down the corridor to find Lord Falcon. They followed closely behind. They were returning home, but it wasn't how Izzy wanted to leave things with the elves. It seemed that she was their only chance of putting things right now.

24

The Birthday Present

Lord Falcon set Izzy and Orlando down from his falcon near her grandad's cottage, just before teatime. She checked her pocket again to make sure the invisibility potion was safe.

"Now then," said Lord Falcon, "first things first. We must make you normal size again, although I've had a request from the mice to leave Orlando small. What do you think, Izzy?" he winked.

Izzy laughed, but Orlando didn't find it quite so funny.

Izzy and Orlando stood still while Lord Falcon uttered the incantation and flicked his wand. A mist swirled around them and they shot upward, back to normal size once again.

"I've put someone in place to relay messages to and from the palace to keep you in touch with us. You both know him."

Izzy was puzzled and looked at Orlando, who shook his head.

"Do you remember Russell?" said Lord Falcon. "He will be your contact. He's been living in your grandfather's garden ever since you left. You can find him later. Well, I'll say goodbye, I must return to the palace as soon as possible."

"Wait," said Izzy. "What about the spell you cast on Grandad and my parents? Don't you need to alter their memories back?"

"No, no. It's a very clever spell. Just give a reason for being away and it will automatically become their reality.

Any reason you like."

"Anything?" said Orlando with a grin. "How about learning to tame lions at a circus?"

Izzy laughed. "Ooo, that could be fun."

Lord Falcon raised his eyebrows. "I'd stick to summer school, Izzy, or something that is believable at least. Now, I really must go. If there is anything you're worried about, just send Russell with a message. Farewell, Izzy. Farewell, Orlando."

He swung himself up on to his falcon and flew into the evening sky. They both waved goodbye, watching him go.

Hurrying down the path towards the cottage, Izzy realised how pleased she was to be seeing her grandad again. She ran into the kitchen where he was sitting at the table having a cup of tea. He looked at her with a puzzled expression on his face.

Izzy hesitated for a moment – although it was a little ordinary it was probably best to follow Lord Falcon's advice. "Hi, I'm just back from summer school, Grandad. You remember, don't you?"

"Oh yes, are you back already? My memory seems a bit fuzzy for some reason."

Izzy smiled and gave Orlando a secret look.

"Grandad, will Mum and Dad be down for my birthday tomorrow?"

"Birthday …? Of course, it's your birthday tomorrow, isn't it? Whatever is wrong with my memory today?" He scratched his head with a bemused expression on his face. "I'll phone them now and check they're coming for lunch."

Izzy went to bed feeling much happier than she had been for the previous few nights. She knew things appeared bad for the elves, and that friendships had been torn over the right to distribute magic, but she was sure she could help. She was sure she could put things right again. Orlando took his place at the bottom of her bed, padded the duvet several times, and settled down, purring contently.

As she drifted off to sleep, Izzy started to mumble once again. "Nanny Ellen, please help me to help the elves, please help me to help …"

In the morning when Izzy woke, her memory was still clear with a dream so vivid that she knew it must be a message from her grandmother.

"I'm getting better at this," she said to Orlando, who was waking up with a stretch. "I just wish I could see Nan when I'm awake, not just in my sleep. I miss her so much."

"What did she say?" asked Orlando, making his way over to her lap, purring happily.

"In my dream, I was standing beside Nanny Ellen in the lift in St Onomans. We went up to the sixty-fourth floor, and then we climbed the last couple of flights to the penthouse suite. And then something important happened; there was something I had to see, something by the window … that's when I woke up."

"That's a good start," said Orlando. "Hmmm, of course I'm sure I'll think better after some food."

Izzy laughed. "C'mon then, Puss. I should know better than deprive you of your breakfast. Then we'll go and find Russell."

They scampered downstairs where Grandad Jim was busy cooking breakfast.

"Boiled eggies and Marmite soldiers?" he said, popping two large eggs into a pan. This one is from Marigold and this one is from Blanche, they laid them especially for your birthday this morning."

"Oh, Grandad," cried Izzy, as she saw her present on

140

the table. It was beautifully wrapped in red, shiny paper with a large gold bow on the top. She tore open the package and gasped in delight. "It's the wildlife book I wanted. Thank you, Grandad."

Izzy and Orlando spent a pleasant morning in the back garden with Russell, filling him in on all the news, and it was just before lunch when Izzy heard the sound of tyres on the gravel outside.

Her parents pulled up in their black Range Rover, and Izzy rushed through the cottage and out of the front door to greet them. She was hoping her mother had come dressed sensibly for the country, but was exasperated when she tottered up the garden path in a designer dress and high heels.

"Happy birthday, sweetie," her mother gushed.

"Happy birthday, darling," said her father, picking her up and swinging her round. "Have you had a nice time with Grandad?"

"Yes, I always love it here."

"Have you made any new friends at Summer School?" said her father. "I hope you haven't been spending too much time shut up with Orlando."

"Actually, I have made a few new friends," said Izzy, as she thought of the elves.

"Good, I hope we can see them sometime."

"I hope so too, Dad. Although you can see them anytime you want, *if* you believe."

"Good, I'm pleased to hear it. Now, Mum thought it would be a good idea to take you somewhere special. You know, like a safari park or something … completely your choice."

Izzy pretended to think for a moment. "Can I go to work with you, Dad? I wasn't interested at first, but I'd like to see what you do now."

Her father looked puzzled. "No, I meant somewhere nice. You'd only find work boring, darling."

"You said it was my choice. I want to know why you work so hard. It might help me to understand. I really want to, *please, please,* will you take me?"

Her father looked at her mother, who was just as puzzled, but gave an approving nod.

"Well, if you're sure that's what you want. We could go tomorrow. The Chief Exec did say you were welcome back anytime. But I won't be able to stay with you the entire time; I'll have meetings and things to do."

"I don't mind, I'll be fine." Izzy congratulated herself on how easy that had been.

After lunch they went for a walk, and Izzy gave a sigh of relief when her mother took her wellies out of the car. They were designer wellies, of course, but at least they were more appropriate than high heels for walking in the country. While her mother was struggling to pull them on, Izzy called Orlando. He came trotting out and without any fuss let Izzy attach a lead to his collar.

"We're ready when you are," said Izzy.

"Don't you find that strange, Liz?" whispered her father, as Orlando walked along with them.

"Our daughter certainly has a rapport with animals," her mother whispered back, "Perhaps she'll make a good vet."

Izzy looked around to see her father half-smiling, deep in thought. He awoke from his trance, and waved.

Grandad and her mother made Izzy's favourite meal for a birthday treat, tagliatelle with Bolognese sauce and green salad, followed by home-made coffee ice cream. And, even though it did seem a little childish now she was twelve, there was the compulsory birthday cake.

"Blow out the candles and make a wish," said Grandad

142

Jim.

It was covered in marzipan animals too. How old did they think she was? Izzy smiled, it was a kind thought. She took a deep breath, blew out all the candles in one go and made a wish.

"What did you wish for, sweetie?" said her mother.

"It has to be a secret or it might not come true, Mum." Izzy was in such a good mood, she didn't mind playing along with the silliness.

The next morning Izzy's parents got up early to return to London. Izzy was woken, too, and got washed and dressed as quickly as she could. Her father watched in amazement as she calmly walked out the door with Orlando on his lead and collar.

"No, I'm sorry, Izzy, but the cat is not coming to work with us."

"He'll be perfectly well behaved," said Izzy, smoothing his great head while he purred.

"No, I could lose my job if he gets loose."

"I'll put him in my backpack when we arrive. Nobody will even know he's there."

"Let her take the cat," said her mother. "He does seem an amazing animal. How many other cats do you know that can go for a walk on a lead?"

"No, and I'm really sorry about this," spluttered her father, "but absolutely not. Under no circumstances can the cat come with us. No. And that's my last word on the matter."

Izzy knew that her father's last words were rarely ever final, and she had the whole drive there to change his mind.

They dropped her mother off at Yvonne St Claire, the fashion house where she worked, and carried on to the car park that was closest to St Onomans.

"Promise me you'll keep that cat under control, Izzy, it is very important." Her father looked defeated.

"No-one will even know he's there," she promised, feeling well-pleased with herself.

She slipped Orlando into her backpack as they approached the main doorway. Marco, the head security man was on duty again.

"Hello again, Izzy," he said, smiling a welcome.

"Hello, Marco," said Izzy, and waved as she followed her father into the lift.

"I'll show you around my department first," said her father as they made their way along a corridor with wooden doors that had shiny, brass nameplates. "You'll be able to see the sort of work I do. It's in development, mainly … identifying run down areas with potential, where we can build hotels, marinas and new roads."

"What does that mean exactly, Dad?"

Izzy's father got very enthusiastic as they entered his office.

"I'm working on a project on an island just off the south coast, at the moment. It's very important to the Chief Exec to push this one through. An old lady owns the land we want to develop, but she won't sell, even though we're offering more money than it's worth."

"Perhaps it's her home and she loves the place," ventured Izzy, lifting Orlando out of her backpack.

Orlando settled down comfortably on her father's desk and started to groom himself, much to her father's disapproval.

"But that doesn't make any sense," said her father. "She would become very wealthy by agreeing to the sale, and it would make a lot of jobs for people."

"Money isn't everything. And some people aren't

greedy, Dad."

Her father looked slightly exasperated.

"You can't stop progress, Izzy. Look, these are the plans."

Her father took some papers from a drawer and spread them out on the desk. One of the papers was a map of an island. The bay where the development was planned was marked clearly. There was an artist's impression of how the bay would look after the work was finished. Hotels, shopping malls, and a marina were planned. Izzy looked casually at first, but then became startled. Her stomach swooped, and her heart pounded in her ears. She studied the map closer, it couldn't be …

Izzy had to find out more. She decided to change tack. "I must admit it does look wonderful in the drawing, Dad. You said it was important to the Chief Exec, do you know why?" She tried to hide her concern.

"I'm not really sure. He just said he had a personal interest in developing this area. A bit unusual actually, it's small fry for him. I guess he must have other things planned, as well."

Izzy nodded as her father talked, but her mind was racing. Was this the bay where the palace was? It looked too similar to be a coincidence. She had to get a copy of the map, the photographs, and the drawings, and take them to Ornella.

"I've got a meeting now," said her father, "just for an hour. Will you be all right on your own?"

Izzy glanced at the documents spread out on the desk. "Ummm, yes, Dad. We'll be fine. Ummm, I've brought my new book to read, we'll be fine."

Izzy pulled Grandad's present out of her backpack and pretended to settle down.

"I'll organise some refreshments for you. Promise me

you'll keep Orlando safe? Please, Izzy, you won't let me down, will you?"

"Ummm, yes, Dad, I promise." She opened up her book, trying hard to look innocent and unconcerned.

This was her chance. If she was going to do something, it had to be now.

25

A Nasty Shock

Izzy looked over the top of her book as her father left the office. He closed the door behind him and she slipped over and cracked it open again, watching to see where he had gone. "Orlando, this looks really bad. I must get copies of these to show Ornella."

"I agree, but how?"

"I thought I saw a photocopier in the main office," said Izzy, peering through the opening. "If only I could use it without being seen. Oops, someone's coming." She closed the door, and sat back down.

"Leave it to me," whispered Orlando, as a young lady came in with a tray of drinks and biscuits.

Orlando started to purr outrageously, and swished his tail across the woman's arm. "Meow, meow, MEOW," he said, and tipped his head to one side and smarmed himself against her.

The young lady squealed with delight. "Oh you are a handsome cat, yes you are." She smoothed his coat enthusiastically. "I have two cats of my own at home. What's your name?"

"His name's Orlando," said Izzy. "And I'm Izzy."

"I must tell the others." The young lady rushed out of the office and called to three of her colleagues to come and see. As they piled in to the small office, Orlando winked at Izzy, and while they were busy making a fuss of him, Izzy slipped the documents off the desk and made her way to the photocopier. When she returned, Orlando was still playing up to them superbly, rolling on his back and letting them tickle his tummy. They didn't even notice when she slipped the copies into her backpack.

"Well, we must get back to work I suppose," said the young lady with a sigh. "You can come and visit us anytime, Izzy. Bring Orlando, too."

Izzy smiled and waited 'til they'd gone. "Well done, Puss. You certainly got their attention."

"I guess I had to take one for the team," said Orlando.

"Don't give me that, you loved every minute," said Izzy, laughing.

"I'll have you know, being this charming takes a lot of effort. Anyway, how would you like three strangers putting their grubby hands all over you?" He started to groom himself all over again.

"I might have believed you, if you hadn't complained so much," she said with a chuckle. "Anyway we aren't done yet, I still have to get a look at the penthouse."

"Aren't the photocopies proof enough?"

"Without evidence that the goblins are behind it, they don't prove anything. I have to get to the bottom of this, too much is at stake. I have to get up to that penthouse." Izzy looked at her watch, "Dad won't be back for at least another half hour, this is my best chance." She looked for the little phial in her backpack and the note with the ancient words.

"Can I come with you?"

"Sorry, Orlando. There's only enough for one. You're going to have to stay here, and keep out of sight."

She took a deep breath then drank the potion in one gulp. She felt a sweet, fizzing sensation on her tongue, the taste of aniseed and vanilla, followed by intensely salty anchovy.

She gagged a little, "Yuck, this stuff is vile."

Orlando flared his nostrils and sniffed the air, "I think it smells quite nice. Are you sure there's not anymore?"

"It's not a cat treat, Orlando." She quickly said the incantation and waited. "I don't feel any different. How long do you think it takes?"

"I'd say right away. I can't see you."

"Okay, I guess this is it. Wish me luck."

She walked out of the office very cautiously, but no one seemed to pay her any attention. She waved her arms about to make sure. No … no reaction. Feeling more confident, she hurried to the lift. It took an age to come from the ground floor. Once inside she pressed the button for the sixty-fourth floor, just like in her dream. It bumped to a halt, and she stepped out into the corridor. It was empty, but somehow she felt her grandmother was there with her.

She walked up the last two flights of stairs until she came to a door. It was marked

SIXTY-SIX
PENTHOUSE – PRIVATE
Emergency Fire Door

Tiptoeing as softly as she could, she stood and listened. Everything seemed quiet. Very cautiously she pushed the handle down and pulled the door ajar. As she felt the draft of air from the room she shivered, it seemed a lot colder than she remembered. Then she saw the stones, six giant monoliths standing in two rows. She shivered again. Dank and foreboding, this place wasn't just *like* a cave, it *was* one.

She made her way into the room, and very carefully closed the door behind her. She remembered about the window from her dream, there was something by the window she had to see.

She started to tiptoe across the room when she suddenly

heard her grandmother's voice in her head. *"Hide, now, Izzy."*

She looked around, there was nowhere to go – the stones were the only cover. Even though she was invisible, somehow it felt safer than standing in the open. She dashed behind one, just as a secret panel slid open in the wall. The sound of footsteps on the stone floor echoed around the room. She didn't dare look, but the voice was unmistakable, harsh and guttural, it was the Chief Exec himself.

"I need you to keep the pressure up on McAllister, send him another memo. Make sure he knows the importance of keeping Green on his toes. I want the island deal to go through quickly."

"Why don't we just send McAllister to the island, sire?"

"Because Tom Green is a nice man, the old lady wouldn't sell to McAllister, you fool. He hasn't got the same credibility. AND DON'T CALL ME SIRE, IMBECILE."

Izzy could hear the voices moving towards the window. She summoned the courage to peep out from behind the stone. There were two short figures in smart suits, the light from the window casting them in silhouette. She couldn't see clearly, but there was something not quite right ... their shape.

Then one of them moved slightly, blocking the streaming sun from the window. She caught a glimpse.

Their heads were green. Clumps of straggled, wispy hair hung over their collars. Then she saw the ears, large, pointed, and grotesque. Goblins.

She suppressed a gasp.

The Chief Executive was halfway through the sliding windows. A waiting helicopter stood on the roof outside.

He stopped, and turned. Izzy saw his face for the first time, it was hideous. He surveyed the room. His beady eyes peering out from his large, green, lumpy face. He sniffed the air with his hooked, pointed nose.

"Did you hear that?" he snarled.

"What? I didn't hear anything, sir."

"Good. The meeting with Thodrek is scheduled for Wednesday. The Green child is becoming a problem though. The minute her father gets that contract signed – deal with her."

"Yes, sir, of course, sir. People go missing every day," the goblin said nastily.

Izzy couldn't help it. She drew a sharp breath; then quickly clapped her hands over her mouth.

"There. I heard it again," said the Chief Executive, stopping once more.

"I'll go back and take a look, sir."

The underling rushed back through the sliding window. He looked around the room, which appeared to be empty, but he continued to search, to feel, to sniff.

Izzy still had her hands over her mouth and was still holding her breath. The goblin moved closer, snuffling his way towards her. His nose was almost touching her hair, sniffing and tasting the air.

Izzy's legs were shaking so much she couldn't run even if she wanted, she was sure to be caught.

Suddenly the goblin sneezed.

A fine mist of snot drenched Izzy's head. For a split second her outline shimmered in the sun, but the goblin's eyes were closed. He pulled a large, spotted, red and white handkerchief out of his pocket and blew his nose loudly.

"HURRY UP," called the Chief Executive. "I haven't got all day. Is there someone there or not?"

The goblin jumped in fright, quickly putting his

handkerchief away.

"No, sir, it's all clear, sir. There's no one here." He stopped sniffing and ran back as fast as he could.

The two goblins scrambled into the helicopter, which lifted off almost immediately, and swung out into the clear blue sky over London, speeding away to the south.

Izzy sank to the floor. Her legs were like jelly and she could feel her heart pounding in her ears.

"Oh my God," she whispered. "What am I going to do?"

Somehow she summoned the courage make her way out of the penthouse. She staggered back down the stairs and into the lift. When she arrived back at her father's floor she walked down the corridor in a total daze. She stumbled into a young woman's desk and sent a pile of papers flying across the floor.

"I'm sorry, I'm so sorry," she said without thinking.

The woman looked around frantically. "Who said that?"

Izzy suddenly realised she was still invisible and crept off as quietly as she could. Finally she made it back to her father's office and invoked the incantation to cancel the spell.

She was about to tell Orlando everything that had happened, when the door swung open and her father came in.

"Everything all right? Did my assistant look after you?"

Izzy was still trembling. "Oh yes, Dad, everything's fine."

"Jolly good, and guess what? Mr McAlister said I can have the rest of the day off." Her father paused. "Are you sure everything's all right? You look very pale."

Izzy didn't know what to say, she just wanted to get out of there. "Maybe I just need some fresh air; can we go home now, Dad?"

That evening, much to Izzy's dismay, her parents had booked a surprise trip to 'The Lion King'. Any other time she would have been overjoyed at such a treat, but all she wanted now was to get back to the cottage. She had to get a message to Ornella.

Izzy went up to her bedroom to get changed, and Orlando raced up after her.

"Of all the times my parents want to spend time with me, this is the worst," she said.

"You know, I wouldn't mind seeing 'The Lion King' myself," said Orlando. He looked at his claws and idly flicked them one by one. "What's wrong, didn't you get the proof you needed?"

"Oh, I got the proof all right, there's no doubt that goblins run the company," cried Izzy. "But they're planning to kidnap me, or worse."

Orlando's hackles rose up.

"What? You need to tell Ornella. We need to get back to send a message?"

"Tell me about it. It'll be tomorrow now, with any luck. This is one of the best birthdays I've ever had, and the worst."

Her father's voice carried up the stairs. "Are you nearly ready, Izzy?"

"Give me a minute, Dad." She slumped on to her bed. "Oh, Orlando, I wish I hadn't stopped Ornella now. She was right."

"But you said it yourself – she could've started a civil war. And she didn't have any evidence. Ornella only wanted to attack the goblins because she hated them. That's no better than the goblins. Trust me, you did the right thing."

Orlando snagged a tissue in his claw and held it up to Izzy. She blew her nose.

"I suppose you're right. I always thought the difference between right and wrong was like in the movies, easy to see. But it's not like that, is it?"

Orlando purred, pushing against her hand, "No, it isn't. Sometimes you have to pick a side, even if they're not perfect. And no one's perfect ... except for me of course."

Izzy managed a smile. "Perfectly naughty perhaps."

"The only people that haven't done anything wrong are Agnes, Gillie and all the creatures on the beach," said Orlando. "And whichever side wins, they're the ones who will have to live with the consequences."

"Oh my goodness, what about Agnes?" said Izzy. "If the goblins planned to kidnap me, what have they got planned for everyone else? I don't believe for a second that they mean to provide magic equally."

"Tomorrow is Tuesday, if we can get your message to Ornella by then it will be in plenty of time for the meeting. Don't worry; everyone will see the goblins for what they are. The proof we have will change everything."

Izzy gave Orlando a big hug just as her father called her again.

"I'd better go, Puss."

As she made her way downstairs, she could hear her parents talking.

"What's wrong, Tom?" said her mother.

"Nothing. It's just that she's talking to that cat again."

"She always talks to him, you know that."

"Yes, but that's not what worries me." He ran his hand through his hair. "I could swear I heard him talking back."

"Perhaps Izzy's right, dear, and you have been working too hard. You'll be seeing little green men next, or even worse, fairies."

26

Equality for All

Agnes wandered through the crowd of creatures that had besieged the bay that surrounded the Ljosalfar palace. There was almost no space left on the beach. She pushed her way past different groups, squeezing into any opening that formed. Finally she saw a group of wood elves, just the other side of some Cofgodas. She shoved past them to join the elves, who were just as excited about the prospect of equality of magic as she was. Agnes eagerly introduced herself. With so many in support of the idea, this had to be right. She wondered if Gillie would come to his senses, or continue being a fool in support of the nobility.

A rumour circulated around the beach; a last minute change of plans, the Goblin Chief Executive was coming - the meeting with King Thodrek had been brought forward to today. No one knew who had started the story, but the excitement was tangible. The crowd surged forward into the palace and up into the Great Council chamber. They swept past Elander's guards, who were powerless to stop them.

Agnes was carried along in the crush. She fought hard and managed to jostle her way to the front so she could see what was going on.

The mood of the crowd was disgruntled, more than ready to hear of all the benefits the company could offer. Agnes could feel the tension building all around her. The atmosphere was electric.

And then she saw the Goblin Chief Executive standing beside the king. The elves had obviously used magic to reduce his size. He was resplendent in his pinstripe city suit, the very model of efficiency and modernity. It was obvious how out of date and old-fashioned the king looked now. Seraphino Cosmos, the king's chancellor, stood with them, as did Ornella.

The chancellor stepped forward.

"My, lords, ladies and magical creatures, we have with us today the Goblin Chief Executive of St Onomans. He has a proposal for all of us that will bring peace, prosperity, wealth and magical equality for all."

He bowed low and waved his arm in the direction of the Goblin Chief Executive.

There was enthusiastic applause.

Agnes listened intently as a wave of silence spread throughout the crowd and Khaverin Fielderial stepped forward, bowing to the assembly.

"Today you will hear it claimed that we are stealing the teeth, the source of all magic," he began.

There was a roar of disapproval from many, but Agnes stayed silent, eager to hear more.

Khaverin Fielderial held up his hand and the roar subsided. He went on.

"It is true we harvest the teeth now, but we are only doing this because we can do it so much more efficiently. The old fashioned method of using tooth fairies is grossly wasteful. We have mechanised the collection process, but not only that, we have perfected a way of extracting more magic per tooth. 'What does this mean?' you may ask. It means, my friends, that St Onomans is in a position now, to offer unlimited magic, TO ALL."

He paused for the weight of this to be considered.

Agnes applauded until her hands were sore, and as she looked around everyone else seemed to be cheering, too. There were cries of 'bravo' and 'well done'.

Khaverin Fielderial continued. "This means equality of magic for all, but not only that, we are proposing equality of jobs and tasks."

Agnes gasped in delight; this was her dream. The noise was almost deafening now as the sea of creatures stood and cheered.

The goblin turned to a flip chart on an easel behind him.

"What this means in real terms is magical creatures can apply for any job they want, not just forced to do the jobs they are given, or born to. For example if a flower fairy aspired to a job in security, there would be nothing to stop her applying. Or if it had always been the dream of a house elf to become a falcon master, now it would be possible."

With mounting excitement, Agnes whispered to the Landwihta next to her. "I could be a warrior at last."

The Chief Executive pointed to a lot of figures on a flip chart. They looked very complex and clever. Agnes didn't have a clue what they meant, but she was impressed nonetheless. He flipped over the page and on the next piece of paper a pie chart could be seen in bright colours, showing how magic was to be apportioned.

"Are there any questions?" he asked.

"Who will tend to nature if we do other jobs?" someone shouted from the back of the chamber.

"I can assure you, nature will be looked after in new ways by inspiring humans with innovation and technology through their dreams. This way the humans will benefit materially too, a much fairer payment than a pleasant dream for a tooth," said the Goblin Chief Executive.

"When will we get our magic back again? We can't fly, we aren't invisible anymore, and we can't do our jobs because we can't go back to our homes," called another from the crowd.

Agnes twisted around but she couldn't see who was speaking.

"Be patient, as we speak machines to distribute magic are being set up all over the country. Go home now, have faith, it won't take long."

"Faith is all very well," cried out a young flower fairy next to Agnes. "But how do we get home safely? It's too dangerous, humans can see us."

"That's easily solved. My company has brought enough magic for a small share for each of you. More than enough to get you home safely."

Agnes joined in the clapping and cheering once more, while the Goblin Chief Executive bowed to the crowd again, then stepped back level with King Thodrek.

Seraphino Cosmos turned to the king. "Perhaps as everyone is here we should take a vote on the matter, Your Majesty? Or do you have anything to add?"

"Take the vote, Chancellor," said the king wearily.

Even from her place within the crowd, Agnes could see Ornella's eyes flashing.

"WAIT!" Ornella cried. "I have something to say."

She stood up and addressed the assembly.

"I have had personal experience of what happens to ordinary creatures when they are corrupted by greed. Have you all forgotten so soon about the seagull attack upon my person? The same thing happened when we tried to negotiate a passage through the Menai Straits. We were captured and held for ransom by the King of the Dokkalfar."

As Agnes heard the gasps of dismay from the assembly, she worried that Ornella might sway the crowd. She felt her dream slipping away.

"Not only that," continued Ornella, "the King of the

Dokkalfar had several shards of children's teeth set in his crown, given to him no doubt by St Onomans. He abused the magic by using it to attack me without provocation, and I was forced to defend myself."

Unable to contain herself any longer, Agnes spoke up. "I was there. I know what happened. It was just one isolated instance of magic abuse by one evil king. We can't let that spoil all the benefits the new company will bring. It's time for equality of magic and equality of jobs. For years now we have been second-class citizens, with the higher magic being the exclusive right of the nobility. I've seen the wastefulness of the nobility at first hand. We need change." She glared in defiance at Ornella.

Ornella went red and there was a general muttering in the crowd, while a few voices could be heard saying, "Hear, hear".

Then someone shouted, "CHANGE." Slowly, the whole crowd took it up and started to chant, over and over again, "Change, change, change."

"CHANGE," shouted Agnes, now completely in thrall to the Goblin Chief Executive and the mood of the crowd. She could almost taste the victory, and to be there, in that crowd and be part of it, sent tingles up and down her spine.

Ornella had lost the argument. As she turned to leave the platform her head was dropped in defeat.

"YES," said Agnes to the Landwihta by her side. "This isn't just a case of who provides the magic from now on. This is the beginning of a revolution."

The vote was a foregone conclusion. Everyone hurried back out to the beach, anxious to get a share of magic to get them home. Without exception, they were all sick of having to camp out on a bare beach with nothing to do.

Agnes looked around for the Goblin Chief Executive.

She couldn't find him, but she saw one of his underlings deep in conversation with Seraphino Cosmos. She hurried up to them and introduced herself.

"Excuse me, but my name is Agnes Ash and I've always wanted to be a warrior. I'm just a wood elf, but I heard the Chief Executive say we would all get the chance to choose the job of our dreams." Her words came out all in a rush and she felt a bit foolish.

Seraphino Cosmos looked her up and down.

"You're one of Princess Ornella's friends aren't you?"

"Um well, yes. Or I was," said Agnes, feeling slightly embarrassed. She noticed his rather leering smile, but chose to ignore it.

"Take this young lady back to headquarters," he told the assistant. "I'll speak to the Chief Executive about finding her a suitable job. Perhaps as a security guard? With hard work I'm sure an elf with your enthusiasm could easily be head of security one day."

"Oh, thank you. Thank you so much," said Agnes, overcome by the ease with which she'd got her heart's desire, after years of writing to the palace begging for a position with the Royal Guards and being ignored.

She followed the executive to the shoreline, where he summoned a seagull.

"Take this young elf to the rendezvous for the train back to Redcliffe Manor," he ordered.

As Agnes climbed onto the seagull's back, she suddenly had a bad feeling about going off like this. She looked back to see if she could catch a glimpse of Gillie, Gavin or Ornella, but there was no one on the beach that really knew her that well.

"Oh well," she muttered. "I would have liked to have said goodbye to Gillie, at least."

The seagull took off, squawking loudly. Agnes held on

tight and took one last look back. She saw Gavin come out from behind a group of rocks; he was running after her, now knee deep in the shallow water of the bay. He was calling and waving his arms.

She turned her head away and wiped a tear from the corner of her eye.

"Pull yourself together," she muttered angrily.

27

Agnes, Living the Dream

Agnes and the seagull landed some way along the coast on the mainland. There were small groups of fairies and elves standing around waiting to be taken away by train.

"Are you all going to the Manor as well?" she asked.

"Yes. My friends and I can't return home because the pesticides the humans are using are choking us," replied a flower fairy. "And the goblins told us we have to pay off the magic we've already received."

"Pay off the magic?" said Agnes, puzzled.

"It's in the small print on the leaflets," said an elf. "You can have as much magic as you like, but it all gets recorded against your name, and if you don't pay it back within the month, they add interest."

"I didn't understand," said another elf looking worried. "I took so much magic that I have to take any job I can, otherwise I'll never pay it back. The goblins said there are jobs we can do in their factory helping to extract the magic from the teeth."

"It's not exactly how I imagined magical equality to be," said the flower fairy.

"So, you can have as much magic as you work for, and the goblins are even offering jobs to everyone. That sounds fair to me," said Agnes abruptly, dismissing the concerns of the others.

One of the Goblin Executives started to herd everyone towards a small bank that was covered in bushes. He disappeared down an opening, where waiting inside the tunnel was the train. It was similar to the one the dwarfs used, without the luxuries of course, but just as fast.

Mile after mile whizzed by, Agnes nearly fell asleep several times with the monotony of it, but at last they arrived. It was getting on for early evening, and she was beginning to get a little tired and hungry.

The executives led the way out of the train, up a steep slope, and out into the evening air at last. The Manor house was in the distance and stood as tall as the giant cedars that surrounded it. Built from deep red bricks, the walls were topped with turreted battlements and decorated with stone gargoyles. It was large and imposing, a fine centrepiece for the beautiful parkland.

The elves and fairies gasped at the beauty of it, but didn't have long to marvel as they were quickly taken underground again. They were ushered into spectacular caverns filled with stalls that had all kinds of luxuries. Agnes opened her eyes in wonder at the trinkets, potions, jewellery and other gewgaws that sparkled and shone under the bright lights.

The goblin in charge told them they were free to buy anything they desired here.

She couldn't believe the colour and diversity of the goods on offer. Many of the items were things that had previously only been available to the nobility.

"Oh, I just love this necklace. I must have it," said Agnes to a fairy next to her. "And look at this. It's like Christmas all the time."

The accommodation caverns were soon reached and the executive showed them where they would be sleeping.

"These are nothing but cells," said a pixie near Agnes. "All that's missing are the bars."

The shock for some at seeing the living conditions was just sinking in.

"Oh, it's not so bad," said Agnes stubbornly. The glitter

of the trading halls was still fresh in her mind.

The accommodation for the workers comprised of nothing more than large holes scooped out of the rock face, each with a curtain that could be drawn across the opening.

Then more goblins arrived with small hand-held machines. One by one they held them against the leg of each worker. Agnes felt a sharp sting as a miniature tag, almost too small to be noticed, was darted under her skin. They scanned the tags to record a different number for each person.

"Why are you doing this to us?" said a shocked elf who was standing near Agnes.

"We have to record when you've worked off your magic credits. It's just like the method humans have in supermarkets. Don't worry, we all have to have one, it's a very efficient system," said the goblin.

Next a big pot of porridge was carried into the cavern by more goblins. Agnes almost felt sorry for them as they struggled in with it. They looked as dejected as some of the fairies and elves, but she managed to shut that feeling out quite successfully too.

By the time Agnes went back to her cave to settle down for the night, although still excited and full of hope, she felt the experience was marred somewhat by the complaints of the others. She was sure she could hear sobbing coming from some of the caves as well.

"No backbone, some of 'em," she muttered, as she settled down for the night.

Agnes lay in the dark, dozing fitfully, huddled in her cloak in an effort to keep warm; she had been tossing and turning for what seemed like hours. Although it was summer above ground, down here it was quite chilly. She wished she'd been allowed to sleep under the stars like she used to.

Suddenly, she felt a hand over her mouth. She struggled to sit up, ready to fight.

"Agnes, it's me!" a voice said next to her ear.

She twisted around, startled to see him, "Gavin! What are you doing here?"

"I came after you to make sure you're all right," he whispered.

"Yes, of course I'm all right," she said impatiently. "Look, I've been given a new uniform and I'm going to be a security guard."

She could see that Gavin was a bit taken aback.

"Ornella and I are both worried about you. This is a terrible place, Agnes. Can't you see that? Come away with me now."

"I'm sure conditions will improve as soon as I start my new job. This is probably just temporary accommodation. I've been waiting all my life for a chance to be a warrior, and now the goblins have given me that opportunity. No one can stop me living my dream."

"Agnes, you're so stubborn. Don't you realise what's happening here? I've spoken to some of the other fairies and elves. They told me they fear they'll never be able to go home because they owe so much magic. Goodness knows how long they'll have to work to pay it all back. Possibly a lifetime."

"I've got no sympathy for them," said Agnes. "They shouldn't have borrowed so much in the first place. I haven't."

"But, Agnes, you have. What about your food and accommodation, this tiny cell, everything? I bet it's all being added to your magic quota. Nothing is given away free by the goblins. And what's that great chunk of glass doing around your neck?"

"It's a necklace and I like it," said Agnes, defensively clasping the red beads. "They're not glass anyway, they're carnelian gemstones mined by the dwarfs."

"What in the name of Freya do you want with a necklace? You're a wood elf!"

"I'm a security guard now. Anyway, everyone is buying things. You don't understand because you've always had anything you want."

"That's not fair, Agnes, I can't help that I was born into the nobility. But I can recognise danger when I see it."

"I'm sure you're just exaggerating things, Gavin. You're only seeing what you want to see. I, on the other hand, have an open mind. I think you must be a Goblinist, too, just like Ornella and Gillie."

"Agnes, nobody could ever accuse Gillie of being a Goblinist, he's the kindest and most unbiased elf I know, and he's very worried about you as well."

Agnes relented slightly. "I know you all think you're trying to help me, and I thank you all, but try to understand, this is what I've wanted all my life. I've made my choice. Please respect it."

Gavin got up and left without another word. He looked angry and frustrated, but Agnes was adamant she was right.

"I know he thinks I'm being stupid and stubborn," mumbled Agnes. "But how would he like being told what to do? I'll show him, I'll *make* this work."

28

The Trap

As soon as Izzy arrived at her grandfather's cottage, she sent an urgent message with Russell to Ornella. She looked out of the window every half hour or so, checking for Russell's return, or for Ornella, or for any word from the palace. But nothing came.

The afternoon wore on into evening, but still there was no sign. Even Orlando started to pace up and down.

Izzy was sitting on her bed, her door closed and a box pushed up behind it to try and barricade it shut. She waited anxiously for help. Then she heard a tapping at the glass.

She looked up nervously at Orlando. "Is it goblins?"

Orlando jumped onto the windowsill. "It's all right, it's Ornella. Goblins wouldn't knock."

Izzy opened the window and a weary looking Ornella climbed through. She flew down onto the bed and collapsed next to Orlando.

"It's all over, Izzy. The goblins moved the meeting to today. Somehow they knew, somehow they are always one step ahead of us."

"But I have the proof, I have the proof now."

"It's no good, Izzy. They've already won, they rightfully control the magic, there's nothing we can do."

Izzy took the maps and photographs out of her backpack and spread them out on the bedspread. "You don't understand, look."

Ornella sat up and leaned across the map. "Why have you got pictures of our bay?"

"I *knew* it was your bay. It's not just about controlling

the magic any more. I saw the Goblin Chief Executive, they are running St Onomans, and they're planning to use the human company to destroy the palace."

"But how can he run a human company?" said Ornella.

"No one ever sees him. He can do everything by computer or phone. I knew something was strange the first time I went up there. But, Ornella, there's something even worse. I think they're going to kill me. I'm so frightened; please take me back with you."

"Oh, Izzy, I'm so sorry. You'd be no safer at the palace. It was just like you said, everyone turned against us. My subjects made a choice, they chose the Goblin Chief Executive, and now we are almost powerless. Even Agnes has gone off with them."

"What?" cried Izzy.

"She went off after the council meeting, along with many others. Gavin followed her., He hopes to bring her back, but I think that's wishful thinking. He'll report back whatever happens. He overheard a goblin say she was going to Redcliffe Manor."

"That's where the dwarfs send the spheres, isn't it?" asked Orlando.

Ornella nodded, "It's their headquarters."

"What if the spheres take the teeth back there?" said Izzy. "Maybe you could get them back?"

"What can we do? The people support the goblins, and if we failed, we would lose everything." Ornella sat with her shoulders slouched, her head down, she didn't even seem like the same person anymore.

"Ornella, what *more* have you got to lose? The palace is going to be bulldozed. You've lost control of your magic, and they could be coming to kidnap me tonight," said Izzy getting agitated. "Take me with you. We might just stand a chance. I am supposed to be the Child of Light

168

after all. We could raid the Manor and take them by surprise. If we fail, it changes nothing. But if we win, what then, Ornella?"

Ornella looked up, "Perhaps you're right, Izzy. I've lost confidence since the people turned against us, but it's my duty to protect them; even from themselves." Her spirit seemed rekindled and her violet eyes flashed once more. "Come, if we are to do this, we haven't a moment to lose."

Izzy nodded. The Ornella she knew was back.

Ornella shrunk the photographs; then Izzy was next.

"WHAT ABOUT ME?" cried Orlando.

"I'm sorry, Puss, you can't come this time. Look after Grandad for me. We should be back before he wakes up tomorrow."

"Time to go," said Ornella.

Regan was waiting in a nearby tree. Ornella gave a low whistle and he flew down to the windowsill. She and Izzy climbed onto his back and they soared into the evening sky. Izzy turned and waved to Orlando just before they flew out of sight.

He stood on his back legs, his paws pressed against the window, his face clearly showing distress. "Please keep safe, Izzy," he called.

Regan flew as fast as he could, spurred on by Ornella as she patted the back of his neck, encouraging him softly. They tore across the sky and arrived at the palace in less than an hour.

As soon as they landed they rushed to see the king to tell him everything Izzy had found out. Then they went to Ornella's apartments, and as they opened the door Gavin was already there, waiting.

"Gavin, you look exhausted. Did you find Agnes?" said Ornella.

"I found her all right," his face was expressionless as if

his soul had been crushed. "She's a security guard, she wouldn't listen to me – she has everything she wants now." Gavin looked up. "What are you doing here, Izzy?"

"We're going on a raid to the Manor to get the teeth back."

Gavin looked shocked for a moment, and then brightened up. "Perhaps that's not such a bad idea. Things there are worse than we thought. Fairies, pixies and elves are all being kept underground like slaves. Magic is freely available, but it becomes a debt that has to be paid off with interest. Some elves already owe so much they despair of ever going home."

"That settles it. We *are* doing the right thing," said Ornella.

There was a knock on the door.

"Who can that be at this hour?" Ornella hurried to open it. "Elander, I didn't expect you. What is it?"

"Princess, forgive me, I was coming off duty when I saw Lord Goshawk arrive. He looked distressed so I followed him. I've been waiting in the corridor undecided whether to talk to you or not. I know something is wrong. I owe you a great debt and whatever the risk, I've come to offer my services."

Ornella looked at Elander. She made up her mind immediately.

"Come in quickly and sit down," she ordered. "Our subjects are in trouble. Gavin has just returned from Redcliffe with the news, and Izzy has confirmed my worst fears about the goblins."

"I thought it was strange that so many fairies and elves were leaving the beach on seagulls. What do you plan to do?" asked Elander.

"We're going on a raid," said Ornella. "Izzy will be coming with us."

She smiled at Izzy, and briefed Elander on the situation. "Look, here are photographs of the bay. Before long, where we're sitting could be a pavement café or marina."

"Have you seen the king?" asked Gavin.

"Yes, he agrees, we should strike immediately."

"There's a good chance the teeth are there," said Gavin. "There's a factory in one of the tunnels where they extract the magic. Even if they're shipped on somewhere else, they must arrive at Redcliffe, first."

"What about Agnes? Will she be with us?" said Ornella looking at Gavin.

"She made it clear that this is the opportunity she's been waiting for all her life." He punched the wall in frustration.

"She doesn't understand the true nature of goblins," said Elander. "I suggest we take a small group of my men. There's less danger of being seen with a small party, and we'll have the element of surprise."

"What about Gillie?" said Izzy. "He's Agnes' best friend after all."

"Yes, you're right. Gillie should come, too," said Ornella. "I can't imagine he'd turn down a chance to rescue Agnes, whether she likes it or not. Now, let's go. We have a long and dangerous night ahead."

Elander stood, ready to go.

"Thank you. All of you," said Ornella. "Remember everyone, not a word of this must leave the room. The king still suspects a traitor in the palace, but who it is, we do not know."

They all hurried on their separate ways, and didn't notice the slight noise of a panel sliding open in the wall next to Ornella's chambers. Behind the panel was a small room, where every word that had been spoken had been overheard. In the darkness of the passageway, a tall figure wrapped in a dark cloak, slipped out, and headed for the beach.

Izzy, Ornella, Gavin, Gillie and Elander with five of his men, were gathered in the Hawk and Falcon Tower. They had arrived at staggered intervals, so as not to arouse suspicion.

"Gavin, you lead the way," said Ornella.

"If we get separated, head for Camberley," said Gavin. "You can't miss the giant fir trees that form two lines across the countryside. The Manor is set in its own parklands very close to them."

They mounted their falcons. Gillie rode with Gavin on Mina, and Izzy climbed onto the back of Regan with Ornella. They took off at intervals, and headed down the coast.

The first few pairs flew slowly until the others caught up. Then they flew on together, in tight formation, into the approaching night. The land took on a rosy glow as the last rays of the sun set behind them.

Even though Izzy knew the mission was dangerous, her spine tingled with excitement as she held on tightly behind Ornella.

It was a long journey and almost midnight by the time they arrived. The falcons set them down in the grounds some distance from the house, then flew off to wait in the trees.

Gavin led them towards the underground accommodation. A gentle breeze was blowing, only the odd hooting of an owl could be heard. It was a perfect night. Izzy felt perhaps too perfect.

"That's where they sleep," said Gavin, pointing to the caves, "Agnes is down there."

172

"Let's go and get her," said Izzy.

"Later," said Ornella, exchanging a glance with Gavin. "First, we must secure the teeth."

29

Betrayal

Izzy followed Ornella and they moved quietly through the grounds away from the accommodation area. The only noise was the wind rustling the leaves in the trees.

"Where are we going?" whispered Izzy.

"To the Manor," said Ornella. "I think that's where they might keep the teeth."

"I agree," said Gavin. "Let's check it out."

They stayed low and skirted around the open parkland, keeping as much as possible to the deep shade and shrubbery.

There was a large rhododendron bush just across from the main entrance. They hid in its deep shadows. Two goblins were standing guard at the main entrance.

Izzy gasped. "They're *huge.*"

"Quite a bit different, isn't it, seeing them from our size?" said Ornella.

Izzy nodded. "They're just as ugly though."

Elander sent his men around the back to check things out. It wasn't long before they returned.

"The only guards are at the front," said Elander, "but there is a guard house at the rear packed full of them. We daren't risk it."

"Then we need to get past the ones at the front," said Izzy.

"I could make us invisible and we could try to slip past, but I don't want to waste my magic," said Ornella.

"I've got an idea," said Izzy. "If Gillie gets them to come over to the bushes we could knock them out."

"You're thinking in human terms, Izzy, they're far too

big to knock out," said Ornella.

"Wait. I have a sleeping draught," said Elander. "It's for pain relief, but if I use the whole lot, they'd be knocked out for sure. But we need to get them on the ground so I can jab them."

He showed them a small dagger with a hollow reed running through its centre.

Izzy looked at Elander's men. "Elander, get your men to tie their rope between the trees. Then, Gillie, you talk to the goblins, and I'll pop out and show myself. They'll chase after me, trip on the rope, and you can get 'em Elander."

"Izzy, you're a genius," said Ornella. "Let's do it. Quickly, tie the rope."

Elander's men secured the rope between the trees, making sure it was stretched tight. Elander filled his dagger with the potion, and nodded to Gillie.

"Go, Gillie," said Ornella.

Gillie sauntered out into the night in full view of the guards. He didn't look at all troubled as he made his way up to them.

"Excuse me," he said in his most polite voice. "I'm just a wood elf, but I've always wanted to be a security guard. Do you know where I can apply?"

The guards looked at each other, amazed, then back at Gillie.

"Um, well," said one, scratching his head. "We dunno anyfing about that. You'll 'aff to wait till mornin', an ..."

"LOOK," cried Gillie, pointing to the bushes. "Look, A SPY."

Izzy jumped out of the bushes.

There was no response from the goblins.

She ran around, and waved her arms over her head.

The goblins looked confused.

Gillie started to run towards her. "We can catch her. *COME ON.*"

The goblins got the idea and broke into a run – loping and clumsy.

Izzy left it long enough for them to see where she was going … then disappeared, running straight under the rope.

The goblins crashed through the bushes, hot on her heels. The first one tripped, and went down so hard he shook the ground. The second one, close behind, fell right on top of the first. Elander leapt onto their heaving bodies, quickly jabbing them both in the neck.

There was a groan, a shudder, and they sank into unconsciousness.

"Good, let's go inside," said Ornella.

Izzy noticed a filthy, smelly toe poking out the bushes as they ran to the house. She didn't suggest covering it up, she might have to touch the disgusting thing. The darkness would probably hide it anyway.

The entrance wasn't locked and they crept inside. To the right of the entrance hall a door was ajar. Izzy peeped inside and gasped.

"They're here, Ornella, the teeth are all here," she whispered, her heart pounding, hardly able to breathe. "A great pile of them."

"Keep watch, Izzy, we'll go in."

Ornella, Gillie, Gavin, Elander and his men entered the room.

"We'll use the magic in the teeth to transport everything, including us, back to the palace," said Ornella.

"Don't forget Agnes," said Izzy.

"I'll go back for her," said Ornella. "Don't worry, Izzy."

Suddenly, alarms went off and bars slid across all the

windows and doors. Izzy stared in horror at her friends now trapped in a prison.

She pointed to the empty room behind her friends. "The teeth are all gone."

Ornella spun around. The teeth had disappeared. "Run, Izzy. RUN." She pulled her wand out ready for battle.

Izzy hesitated, then turned to flee, but too late … a vice-like grip encircled her waist. Terrified, she was hoisted into the air like a rag doll. It was the Goblin King, more hideous than ever close up. She twisted and kicked, trying to get free, but it was no use, his hand was the size of a giant's compared to her.

"Well, well, well, Izzy Green," he said laughing. "Princess Ornella, if you ever want to see this girl again, I'd put that wand down."

Ornella hesitated for a moment, looking the goblin in the face. He squeezed Izzy around the middle. She cried out in pain.

"I'm waiting, Princess …"

"NO. Don't do it, Ornella," called Izzy as she struggled in vain. "Don't give up your wand."

Ornella threw her wand at the goblin's feet.

"That's better," he cackled. "I knew my trap would work, but I didn't expect to get you, Miss Green. Gift sized, too. This is better than Christmas." He held Izzy at arm's length, her legs kicking uselessly at the air.

Khaverin Fielderial stood looking at Izzy's friends through the bars, with a crooked smile on his face, gloating at his victory. "I knew you'd try something like this, Princess, you're so predictable. Don't you realise the vote at the council meeting gives me, and only me, the mandate to control the teeth? Your trespass here is a hostile act; I'm the one with the power now."

"By the fruits of Quercus, if the elves knew the truth

they never would have voted for you," shouted Gillie.

"The truth?" The goblin laughed. "My naïve friend, you still don't understand, do you? People only believe what they want to believe. The truth is, I gave everyone exactly what they wanted, a choice."

"But it wasn't a fair choice," seethed Ornella. "You corrupted them, you only told them what they wanted to hear – you engineered everything from the start."

"Yes, I did, didn't I?" he sneered. "It was easy when I found out about your plans, almost as soon as you made them, in fact. Oh yes, your Chancellor Seraphino Cosmos saw to that. And that little friend of yours, my new security guard, she was a great help, too."

"Agnes wouldn't betray us," said Izzy, gasping for breath and struggling in his grip.

"Oh, but she has already. My company can give her far more than you ever did. She's quite happy in her new position."

"What do you intend to do now?" said Ornella with ice in her voice.

"Whatever I want," said Khaverin Fielderial unpleasantly. "I will bulldoze your precious palace and build a magnificent complex in its place. Plus I have unlimited use of fairy and elf labour for next to nothing. It's amazing what creatures will do for the idea that they have free choice. Running a global corporation beats being a king any day. I haven't even lost my power. Money can buy me anything … or anyone."

"But you can't use the magic," said Izzy. "Only the Ljosalfar can do that."

"A trifling detail, my dear Miss Green," he said, waving Ornella's wand around. "It won't take me long to bribe someone for that knowledge, your chancellor for instance. And as for you, Elander, you could have

178

benefited from the wealth, instead of being a traitor to your brother. He told me all about it. In fact, I can probably raise a few bars of gold by ransoming you back to him."

"You can't do that," said Ornella, thickly. "He'll be killed."

The Goblin King looked at Ornella with scorn in his eyes.

"In fact I might ransom you, too. I believe Ragnestar is looking for a bride, and you might just fit the bill … for the right price."

"Take me if you must, Goblin," said Elander grimly. "But spare the princess and the child. If you don't, I will make you a promise. No matter how long it takes, or what it costs, somehow, I will hunt you down, and kill you."

"Oh dear," the goblin cried in mock fear, raising a hand up in horror, "I'll be shaking in my shoes from now on. And look, they're such nice shoes, aren't they?"

The look that Elander gave the Goblin King would have struck fear into the heart of anyone, but the king was so pleased with himself that nothing could dampen his spirits. He walked away, cackling happily as Izzy struggled and squirmed in his fist.

"What will you do with her?" shouted Ornella, her face pressed to the bars.

"What does anyone do with an annoying little pest?" he said. "Stamp it out."

"ORNELLA," screamed Izzy. "Please, sir, please take me back to my friends."

But it was no use. Izzy's pleas went unanswered.

Ornella slumped to the floor in a faint, and Elander rushed to break her fall.

"This is my fault," said Gavin. "I've put Izzy and the rest of us in danger. I should have known the teeth wouldn't be kept here."

He punched the wall in desperation.

"No, Gavin. We wanted to believe it," said Ornella as she recovered. "No one's to blame but us, it was all too easy."

30

Broken Dreams, Mended Friendships

Agnes was woken by the sound of alarms. She pulled her curtain back. Everyone was milling around in the caves, woken by the disturbance. She went over to talk to a few goblins that were standing by some fairies. "What's going on? Do we have to evacuate?"

One of the goblins laughed. "It's nofing to worry about. Our Chief Exec just 'ad a little surprise planned to catch some vermin up at the Manor."

"*Royal* vermin," said another goblin with a wide grin.

"A vermin princess," said a third, with a sneer. "All right yer pixies an' elves, back to yer beds, otherwise we won't get no work out of yer tomorrow."

Agnes went back to her cave, her mind racing.

"It must be Ornella," she muttered. "It's just like her to launch an attack on the goblins. She's so selfish. She's been waiting to do this since I first met her. I bet she's been captured, and probably Gavin and Gillie with her."

It was too much for Agnes, she'd only just got the job of her dreams. And now her friends had to go and spoil things.

She sat huddled in a corner. It wasn't her problem; perhaps her friends should face the consequences of their actions. But what would the goblins do to them? Agnes tried to block out the thought. Every time she closed her eyes she saw a terrifying image, a glimpse of their fate. She tried to convince herself they would be all right, but deep down she knew what it meant. She held her stomach as it churned in pain.

"Damn. Damn you Gillie, I can't leave you."

Agnes looked down at her leg where the microchip was embedded; if she tried to help she'd be tracked. She didn't hesitate. Taking a piece of cloth, she rolled it up, and bit down on it. She took her knife and dug into her skin.

"There it is," she said as she pulled it out. "I bet Robin Hood never had to do this."

She tried to stand, but felt faint. She sat down again and bandaged her leg, tying it firmly to stop the blood. Then she dug a hole in the floor of the cave and buried the chip.

"That'll keep 'em guessing."

She gathered up her few possessions and hobbled out of the cave. When she reached the surface she breathed in the sweet, fresh air for a few minutes before limping off in the direction of the Manor.

Agnes hid in the bushes opposite the house, almost in the same spot where Izzy and the others had been hiding earlier. There were no guards anywhere, and the main door stood ajar. She ran across the path and slipped in. Then she saw them. Her friends were all in the ballroom, imprisoned in a gilded cage.

Ornella and Elander were deep in conversation. Gillie and Gavin were trying to find a way out, while Elander's men sat on the floor, their heads down.

"Agnes, what are you doing here? You'll get caught," cried Ornella.

"It's all right, I dug out the microchip. They can't trace me now."

"I knew you wouldn't betray us," said Gavin. "You're amazing."

Agnes blushed furiously.

"Never mind us," said Ornella, "Izzy's been taken by the Goblin King, her life's in danger."

"Izzy's here?" said Agnes, shocked. "I thought she

went home."

"Listen," said Ornella. "You must find Izzy and release her. Then find my wand, take her home, and return her to normal size. I will teach you the ancient Ljosalfar words."

"Y ...You're going to trust me with your wand?" said Agnes.

"You've been desperate for one of those – just be careful," Gillie put in.

"Humph," said Agnes, "I'm sure if Ornella trusts me that should be good enough for anybody."

"She hasn't got much choice," Gillie muttered.

"Take this necklace," said Ornella, pulling it from around her neck, and handing it through the bars. "There's just enough magic to change Izzy back."

Agnes slipped the small chain that held Izzy's tooth over her head, and Ornella started to teach her the words.

Agnes repeated them over and over again.

"Are you sure you know them now, Agnes?"

Agnes nodded.

"Good. Get Regan or Mina to tell my father everything that's happened here, including Seraphino Cosmos' part in our betrayal. All our lives may be at risk."

Ornella shot a look at Elander, the distress in both their faces clear to see.

Agnes was about to go, when Ornella spoke again. "Wait. May Freya watch over you, Agnes."

Agnes skirted around the house and entered by the back door. Two goblins were seated at a large table in the kitchen, helping themselves to a snack. One had a cheese sandwich halfway to his mouth, when he saw Agnes. He stopped, mouth wide open, and stared at her.

"Wot do yer want, Squirt?" he snapped.

Agnes paused, trying to think what to do. Then she had an idea.

"Umm, I've come to relieve you," she said. "I'm sure you both could do with a rest after all the excitement."

"Well, I dunno," said the other goblin looking around uneasily. "We're s'posed to watch a special prisoner for the king."

"Okay, if that's what you want, I'll go back to bed," said Agnes, yawning and turning to go.

"Wait!" said the first goblin, and he hastily shoved the whole sandwich in his mouth.

He turned to the his friend.

"She's right. I could do with a rest. Me 'ead's killin' me."

"Yeah. I know wot yer mean," said the second one. "I got a blindin' 'eadache, too. Let's go." He turned to Agnes, "'ere's the key, third door on the left, down there."

Agnes clasped the key to her chest with both arms; her knees sagged with the weight. She waited until the goblins were gone, then checked the corridor. It was all clear. She dragged the key along the passageway until she reached the door, and looked up at the lock. She didn't know if Izzy's tooth had enough power left, but she had to risk it.

She took a firm grip on the key and used all her willpower to lift off the ground. She gritted her teeth as her arms burned with pain at the weight of it. She made it to the keyhole. Then with shaking hands, she used all her remaining strength to turn the key in the lock. She hung on to the handle, braced her legs against the frame, and slowly prised the door open.

Agnes crept into the room. "Izzy?" she whispered.

"Agnes," cried Izzy. She dropped the teaspoon that was clasped in her hand like a club. "Oh, Agnes, I'm so glad to see you." She rushed across and hugged her friend. "Where's Ornella, and the others?"

"They're imprisoned by magic. I can't help them."

"But we must help them. I won't go without them."

"There's no choice. Ornella wants me to get you home; she's told me the spell to make you big. Where's the wand?"

"The Goblin King's got it," said Izzy.

"Oh no. We've got to get it back."

"I … I don't think I can face him again, Agnes." A tear rolled down Izzy's face.

Agnes put her arm around her shoulders. "I'm here now. We'll do it together. Come on, you're the only one who can help us now, we have to do this."

Izzy sniffed. "I'm sorry, Agnes, you're right. I'll try."

"Do you know where he's gone?"

"He said he'd deal with me in the morning, perhaps he's gone to bed."

"Right," said Agnes. "It's as good a place as any to start." She looked out into the hallway. "It's all clear."

31

A Very Risky Business

Izzy and Agnes crept out of the room and into the dimly lit passageway. Everything seemed quiet. Only the faint ticking from a grandfather clock broke the eerie silence. They tiptoed along, keeping close to the wall, and headed for the stairs.

"Voices," hissed Izzy.

Agnes gave a signal to stop, to keep still.

The kitchen door suddenly swung open and a goblin guard looked out. Izzy and Agnes flung themselves behind a small table.

"It's all quiet," said the goblin. "Can't believe the nerve of those two, slopin' off early like that."

"No," said the other voice, "I wouldn't want to be in their shoes when 'He' finds out."

The door closed, and Agnes came out from behind the table, she ran to the foot of the stairs, and beckoned to Izzy. Izzy's heart was thudding in her ears by the time she ran across to join her friend.

They started to climb, each one taking a turn to push, then pull, the other one up, until they reached the top. Izzy was exhausted and sat for a few minutes to get her breath back.

"Listen, can you hear that?" said Izzy.

The sound of snoring was coming from the front of the house.

"Are you okay?" said Agnes.

"I'm all right, let's go."

They edged along until they were by an open door. The

snoring seemed to be coming from inside.

Agnes peered into the room. "It's him." She flattened herself back against the wall.

Izzy took a quick look too, and shuddered. "Do you think he's really asleep?"

The Goblin King was behind his desk, head on his arms. He looked as though he'd been writing before dropping off to sleep.

"It's probably the best chance we'll get," said Agnes. "Come on."

Agnes moved slowly into the room with Izzy close behind. The goblin's jacket was on the back of his chair.

Agnes put her hand in one of the pockets. "Yeuk," she said as she pulled it out. "Snotty hanky."

A breeze moved the curtains. Izzy jumped, on edge. 'I'll try this side,' she said.

She carefully put her hand in the pocket and felt around. It was there. The wand was there. She drew it out very slowly – she didn't dare make a noise. Almost there, almost there, she thought.

The snoring paused. The goblin king snorted, then coughed.

Izzy froze.

Agnes urged her to keep going.

She almost had it, now, just the tip remained.

An owl hooted. She jumped again and dropped the wand. They both watched in horror as it hit the floor. There was a loud snort and the snoring stopped.

Izzy fumbled for it on the ground, she had it. Then a wave of nausea hit her, fear, and panic. She was hoisted into the air, her legs desperately kicking; the vice-like grip of the goblin had her again.

"AGNES. Agnes help me," she cried.

"YOU. Thought you'd trick me, did you?" said the

Goblin King. "Maybe I won't wait until tomorrow to deal with you. You're nothing but trouble."

"LET HER GO," shouted Agnes.

The Goblin King bent down to look at Agnes. "This company gave you everything, elf. I'll deal with you next."

Agnes launched herself, staff in hand, straight at him. He screamed in pain as the pole stuck deep in his eye. He clutched at his face, and dropped Izzy.

"Run, Izzy," yelled Agnes. "Quick, the window."

Agnes snatched up the wand, grabbed Izzy by the hand, and they flew up to the sill.

"What now?" said Izzy. They teetered on the window ledge, a massive drop below them.

The Goblin King bellowed with rage. He pulled Agnes' stick out of his eye and threw it to the floor. Green blood stained his warty face. He staggered to the window, half blinded.

"I'll kill you. I'll kill you both," he growled. His arms flailed as he clawed the air for them.

Terrified, Izzy took a step back and fell. Agnes caught her arm.

"My grip's slipping, Izzy."

"The birds," cried Izzy. "Call our birds."

"REGAN, MINA, HELP, HELP."

The king was almost on them, drawn by Agnes' voice.

A blur of wings and talons swooped down and snatched Izzy out of Agnes' hands. "IT'S REGAN," shouted Izzy.

Mina was right behind. Agnes launched herself into the air and landed on the goshawk just as the Goblin King stuck his hideous head out the window.

He wiped his one good eye, clear. "Enjoy your freedom while it lasts. No one will believe you. *Nothing* can stop my plan – fools."

Orlando was waiting on the window ledge where Izzy had

left him. The sky was just beginning to get light, and the birds were making a racket with their early morning song. As they swooped down low, Izzy saw him stand up, searching for her. Tears welled up in her eyes; she'd never been more pleased to see him in her life.

A few moments later both girls, exhausted and tearful stumbled into the room.

"What's wrong? What's happened?" said Orlando. "I've been so worried."

"Everyone's been captured," said Agnes, and started to cry.

"I must think," said Izzy. She was still trembling, but forced herself to calm down. She began to pace up and down, and then she sat on the floor for a while, her head in her hands.

She looked up at last. "I know, I'll get Grandad to take me to London in the morning. Somehow, I have to get Dad to believe that goblins are running his company. If only I can show him the secret room in the penthouse."

A cold nose nudged her hand.

"Yes, you can come, too, Orlando."

Agnes stopped sniffing and picked up Orlando's tail. She started to dab her eyes with it. He quickly passed her a tissue with his claw, and licked his tail clean again.

"Sorry, Orlando." Agnes blew hard into a corner of the tissue.

"That's all right, Agnes. But I'm glad you didn't do *that* in it."

"Take me with you as well, Izzy. I may be able to help," said Agnes, sniffing.

"All right, but you must stay well hidden. Hopefully, I'll think of some way to persuade Dad on the way."

"I'd better make you big, then. Otherwise, you won't be going anywhere." Agnes took Ornella's wand out of her tunic. "Are you ready?" She started to wave the wand around.

"You sure you know what you're doing, Agnes?"

"Yes, of course. How difficult could it be?"

Agnes started to chant the ancient words. A fine blue mist appeared from the tip of the wand and spread slowly at first, then thickened as it made its way towards Izzy.

"This is really cool," said Agnes.

Then the wand started to shake and bend, almost tearing itself out of Agnes' hand. She clasped it two handed as it took on a life of its own. Sparks started shooting from the end and Agnes was pulled around in a circle. It took all her strength just to hold on.

"What's happening?" cried Izzy, in alarm.

Orlando yelped in pain as a stray spark singed his furry bum.

With a superhuman effort Agnes finished the incantation, and somehow managed to keep hold of the wand. Izzy was returned to normal size.

Agnes stumbled forward, she looked completely drained. She dropped the wand and took a step back, her bottom lip trembling. "M … m … maybe the higher magic isn't for ordinary creatures after all."

32

Trust and a Promise

Izzy and Agnes were exhausted. They were only able to get a couple of hours sleep before morning, but there was too much at stake to stop now. Izzy woke early and listened for her grandfather's unmistakable groaning as he bent down to get his slippers. She rushed into his room straight away and asked to be taken to London.

"This isn't more nonsense about strange notes, is it?" said her grandad. "What's this really about, Izzy?"

Izzy didn't tell him, how could she? In the end her persistent pleas worried him so much that he gave in.

It was mid morning by the time they arrived in London. Grandad parked in a multi-storey car park around the corner from St Onomans, and they walked the rest of the way. Orlando and Agnes were stowed in Izzy's backpack. Both kept extremely quiet, it was probably more than Grandad could handle to have to explain about them, too.

Marco was on duty as they entered the foyer.

"Hello again, Miss Green," said Marco smiling. "Another visit so soon? You must like us here."

"I need to see my dad, it's really important, please," said Izzy.

Marco didn't hesitate, "I'm sure that will be fine, Izzy. I'll sign you in. Do you remember the way?"

Izzy nodded and rushed over to the lifts, with Grandad following close behind. It wasn't long before they reached her father's office.

"I need to talk to Dad alone," said Izzy. "You don't mind do you, Grandad?"

"No, of course not, child," he said, patting her shoulder,

"I saw a sign to a cafeteria in the foyer. I'll be there if you need me."

Izzy marched over to her father's door, knocked, took a deep breath and entered. He looked up, surprised.

"What on earth are you doing here, Izzy? You look shattered. How did you get here?"

"Grandad brought me. I need to speak to you, urgently." She sat down and took Orlando out of her backpack, while Agnes stayed out of sight.

Her father groaned as Orlando rubbed against his legs, leaving a mass of ginger hair on his best suit.

"No, Orlando, no. Bad cat," he grumbled, brushing his trouser leg.

Orlando jumped up onto the desk and settled down.

"Goblins are running your company," Izzy blurted out. "I know it sounds crazy, but it's true. If you don't believe me, just go and see for yourself. There's a secret panel in the penthouse suite, they hide behind it in a special room." She gasped as she got her breath back.

Her father looked stunned.

"You must believe me, Dad. The goblins running the company are threatening to kill me. They have to be stopped."

Izzy's father stood up and went deathly pale. "I'll talk to you in just a minute, darling." He ran his fingers through his hair in an agitated manner. "I've got to make an important phone call." He hurried out of the room.

"Well," said Orlando, "that went down well."

"Maybe I should have got him to the penthouse before I mentioned goblins."

"The goblins bit sounded fine. I think you lost him at 'death threats'," said Orlando. "Well, what's done is done. What do we do, now?"

Izzy looked around the door. Her father was dialling a

number, his fingers frantically pushing the buttons.

Agnes peeped out of the backpack. "Izzy, your father's never going to believe us like this. You have to let me show myself. Even if I'm turned to dust, he may see me for a moment. It could be enough."

"No, no, Agnes, please, I can't let you do that."

"I must," said Agnes.

Tears welled up in Izzy's eyes and she could hardly speak. "Please don't do this, Agnes – I couldn't bear it if I lost you."

"You don't know what I did at the council meeting," said Agnes. "I was the one that called for change. It's my fault everyone is in danger. I have to save my friends, and this is the only way."

Izzy tried to think of something else, some other plan. But Agnes was right, this was the only way.

"Okay," said Izzy. "But if this has any chance of working, he must see you clearly, otherwise it will all be for nothing. Just please wait until I say to come out, I'm going to try something. I love you, Agnes – you're the bravest person I've ever met."

"Braver than Robin Hood?" said Agnes, with a sniff.

Izzy laughed, still with tears in her eyes. "Definitely."

Izzy peered around the door again. Her father was waving his arms about. He was talking to someone on the phone. From the snatches of conversation, Izzy guessed it was her mother.

Izzy's father put down the receiver and came back into his office. "I've just called your mum, she'll be here soon to take you home." Her father noticed the tears running down her face. "Oh, Izzy, don't cry, darling, everything's going to be all right. You really are a worry. It's truly wonderful you've got such a vivid imagination, but you must learn the difference between fantasy and reality.

194

Fairies don't exist. It's all in your mind. Your mother's going to take you to see a special doctor … just for a chat."

Izzy sniffed and wiped her eyes. "All right, Dad, I'll make you a promise. Hold my hands and close your eyes for a few minutes and I'll never mention elves or goblins ever again."

Her father seemed wary as Izzy took hold of his hands. Then he closed his eyes. She knew he was worried someone would see him like this, but she closed her eyes, too, and thought about her grandmother. *Oh, Nanny Ellen, please help me convince Dad that elves exist. Please help me, Nan.* She kept thinking the words over and over again.

A rose coloured mist started to swirl about the room. Then, very faintly, the shape of an elderly woman appeared. She stood just behind Izzy and very gently put her hands on her shoulders. At the touch, Izzy felt a surge of hope and happiness flood through her. The feeling tingled all the way down her arms to the very end of her fingertips and then across to her father's hands. His face relaxed, the worried look disappeared, and he looked years younger.

Izzy knew this was the right time, she felt happy in herself, but more importantly, felt the change in her father.

"Agnes, you can come out now."

Agnes climbed out of the backpack and jumped down onto the table, her legs shaking like jelly, her heart pounding in her chest.

"You can open your eyes now, Dad."

As Izzy's grandmother faded away, her father slowly opened his eyes. Izzy held her breath, not daring to look in case Agnes was turned to dust. She heard a gasp of astonishment as her father grabbed the nearest chair and sat down.

"What on earth is that?" he cried.

He stared at the tiny figure with her fiery red hair, standing on his desk next to Orlando.

"This is my friend, Dad. Her name is Agnes Ash, and she's a wood elf."

"P … p … please, Mr Green," said Agnes. "You must help us. Your company is being run by goblins. The humans must take control again. It would be the first step to helping us defeat them."

Izzy's father sat looking at Agnes. There was no expression on his face – he was completely nonplussed. It was as if he'd fallen asleep with his eyes wide open.

"Umm," said Izzy. "I'm not sure if this is a good time to tell you, but Orlando talks, too."

Her father looked up at Orlando. Orlando lifted a paw and waved. He looked back at Agnes, opened his mouth, paused, and closed it again. At least he was showing signs of life now.

"I, I, I don't know what to say." He finally blurted some words out.

"Pleased to meet you, is a good start," said Agnes holding out her hand.

Very slowly, as though moving through treacle, Izzy's dad held out his hand to the tiny elf. Agnes took hold of his index finger and shook it.

"I'm … pleased to meet you," he said.

"And you have no idea, how very pleased I am to meet you, too," said Agnes.

Izzy suddenly realised she was still holding her breath. She breathed out with relief.

"This is incredible," said her father. He looked at Izzy. "Is this for real?"

She nodded, and smiled back. "I don't know how it happened, but goblins are running your company, Dad."

"Now I think about it, almost everything I do is by memo or Internet," he said, regaining his composure. "I've never seen the Chief Exec … no one has. This is big." He got up and went over to the door. "I've heard of the faceless businessman … but goblins. I have to see this for myself. Izzy, Agnes, stay here. I'm going up to the penthouse."

"No way. I'm coming with you," said Izzy. "Anyway, I know where the secret panel is."

"No, it could be dangerous, let me handle this. I'll find it."

"I have to see this through, Dad," Izzy insisted.

Her father was clearly agitated, but didn't argue any more. They went over to the lift and waited for what seemed like forever. Finally the doors opened and they got in and pressed the large gold button for the penthouse.

Izzy watched the numbers tick over, one by one. They stood in silence, waiting for the doors to open. There was a bump, and the lift stopped. They had arrived on the sixty-sixth floor. They walked into the cold and uninviting penthouse suite once more with nothing but the sound of their feet on the cold, hard stone floor.

33

Ashes to Ashes, Dust to Dust

The penthouse suite looked deserted. Izzy glanced anxiously around the room. Her apprehension grew at the thought of seeing the goblin leader again. She imagined his grotesque face covered with its bulbous warts, but the only thing worse, would be to come so far and *not* find the goblins. What would she do then? She spurred herself on, fighting her desire to leave.

She turned to her father. "The panel is over there on that wall."

"Okay. I'll take a look, but I want you to stay over by the window. I mean it now, Izzy. No arguments."

He went across and searched for the opening, but couldn't find anything. There was no catch, no lever, nothing.

Izzy couldn't watch anymore, and ran over. "It's got to be here somewhere."

She put her head next to a panel. There was a low rumble of voices. Very faint at first, but as she moved along the wall the sound got louder and louder.

"They're here, Dad. I can hear them. Listen."

Her father put his ear to the panel. "You're right, Izzy, I can hear them. Now, I mean it this time, I want you to stay over by the window. I'm going to break in."

There was a small stone ornament on a nearby table. Her father picked it up and started to bang on the wall.

The intercom came on. "Who's there? Stop it at once. I'm warning you, I'll call security." The distinctive rasp of Khaverin Fielderial was unmistakable.

Izzy noticed movement out the corner of her eye. A camera on the ceiling slowly rotated and pitched, until it was pointing right at her. She simply stood, and stared at it with complete defiance.

The intercom sounded again, "IT'S HER, I DON'T BELIEVE IT, SECURITY, COME IMMEDIATELY."

Then more voices screamed over the intercom.

"IT'S THE CHILD OF LIGHT. WE'RE DOOMED," called one.

"We'll all be turned to dust," cried another.

"We'll be killed," said a third.

"Pull yourselves together," Khaverin Fielderial snarled. "Or you'll have more to worry about than some interfering humans. Security will be here any second."

Marco arrived and Izzy watched as he ran over to her father, still smashing on the door. She smiled, and waved at the guard. Marco stopped in his tracks. He looked from one to the other completely bewildered.

"Tom, what's going on? I've just had an urgent call from the Chief Exec. He says there's a madman attacking him."

"You know me, Marco. I'm no madman," said Izzy's dad, and continued to smash the door.

Marco hesitated. The secret panel started to dent and splinter. To one side a small gap began to appear. Three more guards arrived. They ran up to Marco and waited for instructions.

The Goblin King's voice echoed over the speakers once more, "MARCO, YOU FOOL. STOP HIM. If I don't see some action soon, I'll make sure you never work in security again."

There was a pause before Marco replied. "I'm sorry, sir, but it's Tom Green. He said you weren't here."

"IMBECILE. Obviously I am."

Marco gave the order, and the security guards converged on Izzy's father.

Izzy couldn't stand by any longer. She rushed over and caught Marco by the arm. "Please, Marco, don't hurt my dad."

"But don't hurt him, guys," said Marco, casting a worried glance at Izzy.

The guards took hold of Izzy's father, whose hands were firmly wedged in the gap. When they pulled him back, it prised the door open, more and more. With the force of the guards pulling, as well as her father, the door suddenly gave a sickening crack. It splintered at the top, but was still intact.

As they pulled her father away from the secret panel, Izzy knew it was all over. She needed to do something.

She looked up at Marco. "Please. You've got to help us. We have to get in that room. The door needs to come off."

Her hands tingled as she held his arm, and Marco opened his mouth to say something, but suddenly he stopped and looked thoughtful. Then he smiled at Izzy. "That door needs to come off. Jim, Sean, and you too, Rob, give a hand."

"Sir?" said Rob.

"You heard me. Pull that door down."

The guards shrugged, and let go of Izzy's father. They pulled out their nightsticks and levered them into the gap. There was a sharp crack, they heaved, and the door split in two.

The guards all collapsed on the floor in a heap.

Izzy and her father stared into the secret room where pandemonium had broken out on the other side of the door. Goblins were rushing about and bumping into one another. They screamed and yelled at the top of their voices. Some tried to hide under the carpet … some tried to climb the walls.

The Goblin King stood impassively in the middle of the room. With his one good eye, he surveyed the madhouse around him. Then he glared out at Izzy. He raised his arm, and pointed his crooked, warty finger at her.

"LOOK," yelled Izzy's dad to the others. "LOOK AT THAT."

In the moment the guards diverted their attention from the splintered pile of wood, the room was empty. Nothing but dust remained.

The guards stood up, and brushed themselves off, confused as to what had just happened. Adult rationale denied their brief glimpse of the goblins.

"Well, I think the Chief Exec has been playing tricks on us," said Marco. "It must have been an exercise."

Izzy rushed to her father's side.

"Are you okay, Dad?"

"I'm fine, Izzy." Then he whispered, "in fact everything's fine. I saw them. But then they disappeared. I don't understand?"

"They've gone, Dad. That's all that matters. Everything should be okay now."

Her father nodded. "Let's get out of here."

All that remained in the penthouse suite were four very confused security guards and nine piles of dust. Izzy and her dad got into the lift, leaving the security guards still scratching their heads.

"Izzy? Is it safe to come out now?" whispered Agnes from Izzy's backpack.

"Yes, it's all clear."

"Here, I won't need this anymore," said Agnes. She took the necklace with the shard of Izzy's tooth from around her neck. "Take it, Izzy. I'm giving up the higher magic, it's far too dangerous."

"Oh. It's my tooth. It's nice to get it back at last. Right, Dad, here you are." Izzy dropped the tooth into his hand. "Now, what about my money?"

They all laughed.

That night, the cleaning ladies came up to the penthouse suite to do their regular evening chores. They struggled out of the lift with all their paraphernalia. One was dragging a vacuum cleaner by the hose. She plugged it in and started vacuuming the carpet. When she got to the secret room she gazed at the scene in amazement.

"Here, Sheila, come and look at this. Did you know this was here? And just look at the door all broken, I'm certainly not cleaning that up. I don't know what they've been smoking either, but it's green and disgusting. They've flicked their ash all over the carpet. No consideration some people. There's a ring here as well, with a large green stone. It looks expensive – I bet it belongs to the Chief Exec. I'd better hand it in to old McAllister."

Without any more thought, she switched on the vacuum and proceeded to suck up the most wealthy, most powerful pile of dust in the entire world.

34

Endings and Beginnings

Izzy and her father were driving back to Grandad's. In the car with them were Orlando and Agnes. Izzy's dad was still stunned by what had happened, and he ran his fingers through his hair from time to time. Izzy and Agnes chatted happily about how everything would be all right now the Goblin King was gone.

"Regan will carry me back right away," said Agnes enthusiastically. "I can hardly wait to tell King Thodrek the good news, and then we'll be able to rescue our friends."

"Is Grandad Jim still following?" asked Izzy's father.

Izzy turned to Orlando, who was stretched out on the back window ledge.

"Can you see Grandad's car?"

"Meow, Meow," replied Orlando.

"You're talking to that cat again, aren't you?"

"Yes, Dad. And Orlando says please call him by his name. And yes, Grandad is still there."

Her father groaned.

"Dad, did Mum believe you when you said you got mixed up, and I was just writing a story about fairies and goblins?"

"I hope so, Izzy, I really hope so. If she doesn't, she'll think I've lost my mind too." He laughed nervously. "In fact, I've got a hard job holding on to reality, myself. I might have a hard time holding on to my job as well – I did just wipe out the whole of the management board in one go."

"Something that all elves will be forever grateful to you for," said Agnes fervently.

When they reached the old corn mill it was nearly time for the evening meal. Izzy's dad and Grandad made a lovely fry up of eggs, bacon, chips, mushrooms and grilled tomatoes with Izzy's favourite brown sauce.

"Good job Liz isn't here to see this," said her father, laughing, "she'd have a fit, all this unhealthy fried food. We seem to live on nothing but salad at home."

"Yes, Ellen wouldn't have been too pleased either," said Grandad Jim with a furtive look over his shoulder, as if she was watching.

While her father and grandad were busy cooking, Izzy grabbed some food and went out to the garden with her backpack. She called softly for Regan and he swooped down, gracefully landing at her feet.

Agnes climbed out of the backpack and gave Regan a hug. "Good news," she said. "The Goblin King is gone, turned to dust. Izzy got her father to believe in me, and things just sort of happened after that. I'll just have a quick snack and we'll be on our way."

"Don't forget your part in all this," said Izzy, looking at Agnes in admiration. "Regan, you must tell King Thodrek that Agnes was incredibly brave."

"I will be proud to tell him. Now, if you are ready, Agnes, we must be on our way."

"Yes, of course," said Agnes, with a mouthful of bread and cheese.

She waved Izzy goodbye and swung herself onto Regan's back. "I'll be back to see you soon. Hopefully, we all will."

Izzy waved goodbye as Regan lifted off with Agnes. They climbed effortlessly into the gathering dusk of the night sky.

"Hurry up, Izzy," called her father from the kitchen. "Greasy fry up's almost ready."

Before Izzy went back to school at the end of the holidays, she had a visit from Gavin, Agnes and Gillie. They flew in on Regan, Ornella's merlin, and Mina, Gavin's goshawk. Izzy was in the garden pottering about doing a bit of weeding for her grandad. Orlando had spread himself out on the sun lounger; digging really wasn't his style.

"Oh I'm so pleased to see you all," Izzy cried. "What's happened? How's Ornella?"

"The king organised a rescue mission led by Elander's men and there was a battle," said Gillie. "The goblins didn't put up much of a fight without their king, most of them fled or surrendered. Then they were made to release us."

"Unfortunately, there was no sign of the main hoard of teeth," said Gavin. "The tunnels were searched, and only a few piles were found, ones brought in recently by the spheres."

"Ornella and Elander have stayed on to try to restore order and continue the search," said Agnes.

"Oh no," gasped Izzy. "That is bad news."

"The king hasn't got the power to rule the kingdom properly until they're found," said Gillie. "Would you ask your father to look for any clues that might help us?"

"Okay, I'll phone him tonight," said Izzy.

"Actually, Izzy, we have got another reason for visiting you. A much nicer reason," said Gillie. "Do you remember what you wished for at your birthday party?"

"Yes. I always wish for the same thing."

"Well that is your birthday present from the elves. We hadn't forgotten. But it took quite a bit of special magic to achieve it," said Gillie. "And it couldn't be done until we found some of the teeth."

Izzy felt her heart begin to beat faster.

"Go to the bottom of the garden," said Agnes, smiling.

Izzy followed the path down to the bottom of her grandad's garden, her heart racing now. She could hardly believe the elves had granted her dearest wish. As she turned down the path by the old cherry tree, she saw her present. Nanny Ellen was sitting on the bench in the rose arbour, her arms held out to give Izzy a hug.

Izzy ran into her grandmother's arms and they sat and held each other, smiling, laughing and crying. Her grandmother looked just the same as Izzy remembered her.

"I've missed you so much, Nan," said Izzy, tears of joy running down her face.

"I've missed you, too, Izzy," said her nan, wiping her eyes. "Although I do get to see you when you're asleep, and talk to you, too."

"Will I still be able to talk to you in my sleep?" asked Izzy, looking around for her friends.

Agnes, Gillie, Gavin and Orlando had followed Izzy, and they were all smiling at the happiness the birthday present had brought her and her grandmother.

"That will always be part of your powers," said Gavin. "You are the Child of Light, Izzy, the child in the prophecies."

Agnes picked up Orlando's tail and started to dab her eyes.

"Agnes, this is becoming a habit," snapped Orlando, pulling his tail away.

"Perhaps your grandmother can tell you more," said Gavin.

"It's true, Izzy. You are part of the Idesa, as I am too. The name comes from the Old Norse, the Disir. They were women of great power that helped the families they belonged to. In the ancient days many were of nearly goddess level and were worshiped, although a few living mortal women were counted amongst their number. The Disir often appear to members of their families to help, and sometimes to punish. But mostly they appear in dreams. Like when I come to speak to you. They may be called upon to work spells, like when you called for my help at the Bronze Age Circle, and when I helped you to convince your father to believe in elves."

"Why doesn't Mum have these powers?"

"Sometimes the power skips a generation," said her grandmother. "But I could tell as soon as you were born that you were different. You're one of us, quite possibly the last Idesa."

"Why the last?"

"Because the world is changing, people no longer believe in myths and legends, and the old values are being replaced by technology. And although technology is good, it must be used in conjunction with nature and not abused by people like the Goblin King. I believe you will help to make a difference, Izzy, I believe it is your destiny."

"Nan, I don't understand why Marco helped us to break down the door? And everyone keeps talking about my powers, but I don't think I've got any."

"The powers of an Idesa are very subtle, Izzy. It might seem to you that you have done nothing, but it was your influence over Marco that caused him to help you. You almost don't need my help now. But you must be very careful never to abuse that power, or use it for your own gain. The power of persuasion is the most powerful magic in the world."

Nanny Ellen started to fade, and Izzy cast a worried look at the elves.

"It's all right," said Gillie. "You'll be able to see your grandmother every time you come to the cottage. Just come down here and call her name. But it will only be a short visit, a few minutes at most."

"Thank you, thank you all for such a wonderful birthday present. Thank King Thodrek for me please, I know there's a shortage of magic at the moment and I really do appreciate being able to see my nan. Even if it was only for one minute it would be worth it."

"Well," said Gavin, "I suppose we must be getting back to the palace, there is much still to do."

"Yes," said Gillie, "I'm afraid so, but we'll keep in touch."

"You can send messages through Russell," said Agnes. "How is he? I haven't seen him for ages. I'm rather fond of the old crow, I nursed his broken wing once, you know."

They said their goodbyes, and Izzy and Orlando waved as their friends flew off into the afternoon sky.

"I suppose we won't see much of them now everything's back to normal," said Orlando.

Izzy sighed, "I have a feeling it's not quite over yet, Puss."

The End

A History of Elves

Over the centuries elves have been described in many ways, but what is the reality behind their myth? Are they the tall, beautiful, warrior-like beings that look over the destiny of men as described by J.R.R. Tolkien in *The Hobbit* and *The Lord of the Rings*? Or are they the creatures of fairy-tales; the small, mischievous imps that dwell in the woods, in our homes, and all around us every day?

The origin of elves goes back thousands of years to the Germanic tribes of northern Europe called the Anglo-Saxons. They practiced a kind of religion called Paganism, a system of beliefs reinforced and passed on to others through heroic legends, such as *Beowulf*, and mythical folktales, one of which was Norse mythology.

One of the earliest written descriptions of these myths comes from Snorri Sturluson, an Icelandic poet who lived in the 12th Century AD. His collection of stories called *The Edda* describes the elves as follows:

'There is one place there in the sky that is called the Elf Home (Álfheimer). People live there that are named the light elves (Ljósálfar). But the dark elves (Dokkálfar) live below in earth, and they are unlike them in appearance – and more unlike them in reality. The Light Elves are brighter than the sun in appearance, but the Dark Elves are blacker than pitch.'

So the dark elves were evil and the light elves were good. Not necessarily. In the book, *Teutonic Mythology*, published in 1883, Jacob Grimm explains that by the time of Snorri's description, Christian beliefs, such as good and evil, and light and dark, had probably become mixed up and confused with older Pagan ideas. He describes how the mythological Valkyries may have also become combined in this confusion. (In Norse legend, the Valkyries were a kind of warrior goddess that rode into battle to carry the bodies of the slain to the hall of heroes; a place called 'Valhalla'.)

In this way, it is easy to see how the light elves may have taken on the form of the tall warrior-like creatures who resided in the heavens and who battled evil to look over the destiny of men. In the same way, it can be seen how the darker creatures may have become the short, ugly wretches who were forced to live underground, occupying themselves with greed and wealth – goblins, dark elves, and dwarfs, all consigned to mischief and evil – but Grimm describes these distinctions as unjustified and unfair.

Jacob, together with his brother, went on to write a collection of stories called *Grimm's Fairy Tales*, which include *Hansel and Gretel*, *Rapunzel*, and *Cinderella*. But the question remains, was he right about the history of elves?

If he was right and the elves really are magical creatures living alongside us, what would they do if they were living with us nowadays? Would the 'noble' light elves really be so good, and how would years of being portrayed as better than the rest affect the way they behave? Worse still, how would years of being thought of as evil have affected the others? This is a book about REAL elves, the ones you have forgotten about, the ones who you have thought of as grotesque and evil for a thousand years, but after all of that time what have they become ...?

Glossary of names

Alfheimer
(alf-hi-mer) old Norse, meaning 'elf home'

Cofgodas
(cof-go-das) A household spirit living alongside humans.

Dokkalfar
(dock-al-far) 'Dokkr' meaning 'dark', 'alfar' meaning 'elf'

Freya (from the Old Norse, Freyja)
(frey-a) A goddess in Norse mythology, associated with love, beauty, war and death.

Huldrufolk
(hul-dru-folk) Mischievous woodland spirits that have the fronts of men, but the hollowed out backs of trees.

Idesa (from the Old Norse, Disir)
(i-des-a) (dis-ear) Women of great power that are the guardian spirits of their families.

Landwihta
(land-wi-ta) Nature-spirits that are the guardians of the woods, the forests, and the streams.

Ljosalfar
(jos-al-far) 'Ljos' meaning 'light', 'alfar' meaning 'elf'

Nixies
(nix-ees) A water sprite of German mythology, usually in human form or half-human and half-fish.

Svartalfar
(s-var-tal-far) 'Svartr' meaning 'black', 'alfar' meaning 'elf'

Ylfe
(elf) Anglo-Saxon word for 'elf'